# ADVANCE PRAISE FOR
## *Sydney A. Frankel's Summer Mix-Up*

"A book with heart, about finding the bravery to be your true self."

—Jennifer Cervantes, *New York Times* bestselling
author of The Storm Runner trilogy

"Danielle Joseph has created wonderful characters showcasing
humor, sensitivity, and independence, all while highlighting the
importance of friendship. Readers who have enjoyed the humor of
Ramona Quimby will fall in love with Sydney Frankel."

—Christina Diaz Gonzalez, author of
*The Red Umbrella* and *Moving Target*

"I love this book! It's a lovely ode to pure kid friendship, plus it's got
crushes and summer hijinks and dancing. Sydney and her family are
as real and lovable as any you'll find in children's literature. Think
Beverly Cleary's Quimbys or Judy Blume's Hatchers, but even
funnier. Frankelstein power!"

—Josh Berk, author of *Camp Murderface*

"A heartwarming, fun, and funny story about a girl struggling to
fit in. Readers will fall in love with Sydney and root for her as she
navigates the summer program her mom forces her to participate
in before starting middle school. This book is the perfect blend of
humor and heart!"

—Laurie Friedman, author of the Mallory McDonald series

"A warm and funny story that shows just how not alone we are, even
when it feels otherwise."

—Chris Tebbetts, author of *Public School Superhero*
and coauthor of the Middle School series

# SYDNEY A. FRANKEL'S

## SUMMER MIX-UP

**DANIELLE JOSEPH**

KAR-BEN
PUBLISHING

KAR-BEN PUBLISHING®
An imprint of Lerner Publishing Group, Inc.
241 First Avenue North
Minneapolis, MN 55401 USA

Website address: www.karben.com

Illustrations by Basia Tran.

Main body text set in Bembo Std regular.
Typeface provided by Monotype Typography.


**Library of Congress Cataloging-in-Publication Data**

Names: Joseph, Danielle, author.
Title: Sydney A. Frankel's summer mix-up / Danielle Joseph.
Description: Minneapolis : Kar-Ben Publishing, [2021] | Audience: Ages
    8–11. | Audience: Grades 4–6. | Summary: "Sydney is dreading the
    summer course she has to take at the community center-until her best
    friend, Maggie, comes up with a daring switcheroo plan so they can
    both take classes they like" —Provided by publisher.
Identifiers: LCCN 2020030708 (print) | LCCN 2020030709 (ebook) |
    ISBN 9781541598621 | ISBN 9781541598638 (paperback) |
    ISBN 9781728428895 (pdf)
Subjects: CYAC: Community centers—Fiction. | Summer—Fiction. |
    Best friends—Fiction. | Friendship—Fiction.
Classification: LCC PZ7.J77922 Sy 2021  (print) | LCC PZ7.J77922
    (ebook) | DDC [Fic]—dc23

LC record available at https://lccn.loc.gov/2020030708
LC ebook record available at https://lccn.loc.gov/2020030709

Manufactured in the United States of America
1-48030-48731-1/12/2021

TO MY FOREVER LOVES—
DELLE, MARLEY, MAKHI & NAYA.

AND TO EVERY READER WHO HAS FELT
DIFFERENT FROM THE CROWD—WE NEED MORE
OF YOU IN THIS WORLD!

## CHAPTER 1

If I could stay home all summer and read, I totally would. Okay, that's a lie. Watching TV with my bestie, Maggie, would be my first choice. But Mom would never allow that. And who am I kidding? She won't let me stay home and read either. She has *other* plans for me: "Exciting plans that will get you on the right road to middle school."

Yes, she really said that.

Funny thing is there's actually only one road that leads to Coral Rock Middle School. I mean, technically, you could go through the backwoods and risk getting a serious case of poison ivy, but I doubt she meant that.

"Sydney, you're going to be a sixth-grader," Mom reminds me on the first Saturday of summer break. "It's time for you to embrace talking in front of groups, since you'll have to do that in class."

I don't move from my favorite spot on the couch. "I'd rather go to the dentist than spend my summer practicing for class presentations," I say.

"That's not what I'm suggesting." Mom dangles the glossy South Miami Community Center's summer program brochure in front of me. "I just want you to have a positive self-image and feel comfortable in your own skin. No pun intended." She smiles.

I look down at my arm. It *would* be nice not to have red splotches all over it every time I have to speak in front of a group of people.

"I want you to get used to putting yourself out there, trying new things with new people . . . expanding your horizons."

Ever since I wimped out of going to the county spelling bee this spring, Mom's wanted me to work on overcoming my public speaking anxiety. It's hard to believe, but both my pediatrician and my school guidance counselor say that it's within my control.

My plan to control it is to stay home all summer. Why focus on *expanding my horizons* when I could be jumping on Maggie's trampoline, chilling on my couch, and getting used to the new phone that Mom and Dad promised to get me before I start middle school? Maggie's supposed to get hers at the same time—a couple of weeks before the school year starts—which means I'll be able to call and text her whenever I want.

And next year, when my voice gets all shaky in class, I'll tell everyone I have permanent laryngitis. And my cheeks turning red—I'll tell people it's makeup. Magical blush that comes and goes. A new invention. Haven't you seen the infomercial?

"Pick something," Mom says, tossing the brochure into my lap. "Anything. How about tennis?"

"Too sweaty."

"Water polo?"

"I love swimming, but slapping a ball around in the pool? No thanks."

"I've got it!" Mom exclaims as if she's got the winning answer on *Jeopardy*. "Drama. You'll come alive onstage."

"No way, I'd rather die."

"Oh, don't be so dramatic, Sydney!" Mom absentmindedly rubs her round belly.

I sigh and glance through the brochure. And I see it! *Reading Express: The pages come alive as you immerse yourself in stories.* This is perfect! I read almost two hundred books last year. And if I take this class,

I won't have to talk to anyone. I can just hide my face in a book. "You said anything, right?"

"Anything except for reading," Mom says sternly.

Sometimes I wonder if my mother has telepathic powers and is keeping them to herself. "That's not fair!"

"It's a reading *improvement* class, Sydney. You're already a strong and avid reader, so you don't need that. I want you to branch out."

"Mom, I'm not a tree." I stick my arms out and let my hands dangle.

"This is not a joke, Sydney. You can't continue to sell yourself short," Mom says.

"I think it's pretty obvious I'm not short." I plunk my size 10 feet onto the coffee table. It's impossible to forget that I'm a head taller than most of my classmates.

"You know that's not what I meant." She shoos my feet down with a wave of her hand. "It's important that you try something new."

"I'm going to meet tons of people in middle school next year. The summer should be a new-people-free zone." Coral Rock Middle is three times the size of my elementary school, so there will be a lot of new faces.

"*Or* you can use this time to get comfortable with making new friends. Consider it a test run."

"I get it, but I still don't want to go." The brochure says we'll learn how to voice our opinions. I have to voice mine to Mom. "I'll be right back." I run upstairs to my room to grab the list I started the minute she brought up the idea of me taking a summer class. I have no choice but to use it.

Back in the family room, I perch on the arm of the couch and hold up my list. "Listen, Mom. Taking a summer class is a bad idea for a lot of reasons."

"Like?" She motions for me to sit down properly, so I plunk my butt onto the couch.

"Reason One: The community center is old, meaning it's probably full of cockroaches. I'm allergic to cockroaches. I could get a nasty rash. It wouldn't be pretty."

She laughs. "I'm confident that there are no invasive species in the community center."

"Mom, this is not funny." I look down at the next item on the list. "Reason Two: The classes are very expensive. Just one costs the same as buying 1,076 diapers."

"Wow, I never thought of it that way. That's a lot

of diapers." And about four months from now, she's going to need all the diapers she can get.

"Sure is." I lean in a little closer, ready for the clincher. I once watched a real estate sales video with Zayde that talked about how to *seal the deal*. "Reason Three: I could sit next to someone with a very bad virus, and then I'll get the virus and give it to you and the baby." I widen my eyes for dramatic effect. "I'd never be able to forgive myself if that happened."

She opens her mouth to say something, but I quickly add, "And like Dad always says, 'Better safe than sorry.'"

She holds out her hand. "Let me have a look at your paper."

"Um, give me a sec." I quickly review it for mistakes, because the last thing I need is for Mom, the dedicated high school language arts teacher, to mark it up with a red pen. She'd do it too. She gets so giddy when I have a paper to work on for school.

*Giddy* was a word of the day this past month. Every morning Mom puts a new word on the whiteboard in the kitchen. She never takes a break, not even now that we've been on summer break for a week.

Today's word: *agog*. Say it fast, and it sounds like *oh, gawd!* Mom says the words are chosen at random, but I have my suspicions about this one, because it means intensely excited. I think she's trying to tell me something.

Okay, phew, all looks good. I hand the paper to her, pop my feet back up onto the coffee table, and wait for the verdict.

Mom looks up. "Sydney, how many times have I told you to get your feet off the table?"

I pull my glasses halfway down my nose. "Do you want a total count or just for today?"

"Just get them off!"

I flip my feet to the side. "Well, what do you think?"

"Very persuasive. But you're still going to take a class." Mom rubs my shoulder. "Trust me. When you're older, you'll thank me."

"I doubt that," I mumble. I need to change the subject. "Can I go to Maggie's now?" We can't keep talking about this if I leave the house.

She nods.

I'm two steps from the door when Mom says, "Sydney, if you don't pick a class by five, I'll pick one for you."

"Okay." I nod.

"Oh, and one more thing—if you don't complete the class, then no cell phone in August."

"Whaaat?" A dagger pierces my heart. "That's so unfair!"

Mom's arms are folded across her chest. She's not budging.

I look at my watch. It's 4:16 p.m. Less than an hour of freedom left.

## CHAPTER 2

It's now 4:20 p.m. That's forty minutes until dooms-day. Anything can happen in forty minutes. Aliens can land on Earth, pigs can fly, or homework can be banned from the planet, but Mom will never change her mind. Bubbe Rose always says Mom's as stub-born as a stale matzo ball.

And now I'm down four minutes, because that's how long it takes me to walk to my best friend's house. It used to take me four minutes and fifteen seconds, but that was before I grew three inches over this past school year.

Maggie's house reminds me of a lemon. It's bright yellow, and her mom loves Pine-Sol cleaner. Mom used to use Pine-Sol too, but after she found out she was pregnant, she switched to all organic products because breathing in chemicals could harm the baby. Kind of funny, since I've been breathing Pine-Sol fumes my whole life, yet no one ever worried about toxins invading *my* body.

I ring the bell and see one of Maggie's big blue eyes filling the small square of stained glass in the middle of the door.

"It's me!" I wave.

"There are a lot of *me*s in the world. Better identify yourself," she says in a deep voice.

"I'm a spy, and I come undercover. Your people sent me."

"I still need a name."

"Victoria Von Fartstein."

The door swings open. "Nice to meet you, Vicky Von Fart." She laughs.

"Man, wouldn't that stink if that was your last name?" I say.

"Yeah, literally." Maggie laughs again. Her curly hair is damp and much tamer than usual. She's lucky because she hardly ever has to brush it—unlike me with my thick, straight hair that knots up in a second.

Since Maggie's last name is Stein, together we are Frankelstein. We've been best friends since kindergarten, but it took us until second grade to put the two names together.

I follow her into the kitchen and sit down at the counter. "Got any soda? My mom's driving me nuts."

"Sure." Maggie opens the fridge. "Has she banned all flavored beverages again?"

"Worse!"

"Oh, no. Well, it can't be worse than *my* news."

We each grab a soda and head for her room. Maggie's dog, Butter, runs after us and licks my ankle. I crouch down to pet him. "Hi, Butter. I missed you too."

He's a feisty Pomeranian. And for a small dog, he's not afraid of anything. He's definitely Maggie's mini-me.

I sit down at Maggie's big pink desk. "My mom's making me take a class at the community center, and if I don't take it, she's never getting me a cell phone."

Maggie's mouth drops. "No phone?"

"She's making me pick a class from *this*." I slap the brochure onto her desk.

"Don't bother. I've seen it." Maggie huffs.

"What? My mom showed it to you?"

"No." Maggie takes a sip of her soda. "*My* mom showed it to me."

Even worse. "Why would my mom get your mom involved?" I ask. "Is she trying to destroy me?"

"No, my mom wants me to take a class too. Actually, she already signed me up."

"Really? Which class?"

"Reading!" Maggie flops down onto her bed. "Ugh. It's going to stink."

"Not fair!" I pout. "My mom said I could take any class *but* reading."

"You're so lucky." Maggie grabs the brochure from me. "Just pick something else then. Ceramics? You get to play with clay."

"Eh." I shrug. "Remember the bowl I made in Girl Scouts?"

Maggie laughs. "The one that was flat on one side?"

"Yup."

"Then you should take the dance class. That's the one I've been dying to take."

"I would be a total flop in that class."

She pans down the list. "Okay, what about basketball? You'll at least get to be around cute boys."

"You mean sweaty boys." I hold my nose. "The gym has no AC."

"Blech."

I take the brochure back from her. "Study skills: boring. Archery: I'd probably poke someone's eye out."

I look down at my watch. *4:51.* I turn the watch face around so I don't have to stare at it.

"I think there's a science class," Maggie offers.

"I'm done." I cover my head with my hands. "Maybe I'll just borrow your phone for the rest of my life."

"Yeah, but then we can't call each other."

"I know." I sigh. I mostly want a phone so I can send Maggie a thousand emojis.

Suddenly Maggie jumps up from her bed. "I have the best idea."

"What?" Maggie's kind of scary when she gets an idea.

"Syd, hear me out before you say no."

"Okay." I bite the inside of my lip.

"What if we trade places? Like I pretend to be you and take the dance class, and you pretend to be me and take the reading class."

"How's that going to work?"

She picks up the brochure. "The classes are at the exact same time. We can have our parents drop us off out front and sign in without them."

"If my mom finds out, she'll flip. Then no phone. Forever."

"She's never going to find out."

"I don't know." I sigh. "She has a way of finding things out practically before they even happen. It's like a momsense."

Maggie puts her hands together. "Please! You know how much I stink at reading. I want to do something fun. Something I *love* to do. And you love to read, so it's perfect!"

"I don't know. What if other kids from school are there? They'll blow our cover."

"The community center isn't even in our school district," she points out. "And besides, most kids from Coral Rock will probably be at sleepaway camp or on fancy vacations. Pretty please." Maggie clasps her hands more tightly.

I look down at my watch. It's 4:55. Now or never.

"Deal!" I hold my hand up. "Reading Express, here I come!"

Maggie slaps my hand hard. "Yes! Frankelstein power!"

At 4:57, with a whole three minutes to spare, I pick up the Steins' landline phone and call Mom.

"Sign me up for the dance combo class."

"Dance?" Mom repeats.

"Yes," I say before I chicken out of our plan.

"Okay, great," Mom says. "I'm signing you up as we speak."

Please don't let me regret this. What if I get stuck in the dance class all summer? The only place I like to dance is in my bedroom.

"And you're in," Mom says.

I feel a pinch of guilt for lying to her, but I try to ignore it. "Okay." I give Maggie a thumbs-up. She throws back a huge smile.

"I can't wait to buy you a dance outfit," Mom says. "Maybe something silver or gold . . ."

"Uh, I'm pretty sure you can wear whatever you want to the class," I say, grimacing.

"Sure, honey, we'll talk about it." Which translates to, *I'll buy the clothes and force you to wear them.*

But I'll put up with a lot if it means I can secretly take a reading class.

## CHAPTER 3

When I get home from Maggie's, Mom's seated at the kitchen table, talking on the phone.

"Hi." I walk by her to grab a cheese stick from the fridge.

"Hold up." Mom turns to me. "We're having dinner in a few minutes. And Bubbe's on the phone. She wants to talk to you."

I take the phone. "Hi, Bubbe."

"Hi, Sydney. I heard you're taking a dance class!"

Oh, geez, now I have to wear a second layer of guilt? Grandma guilt is even worse than Mom guilt. It's super guilt.

"That community center is fabulous," Bubbe goes on. "Your mom took a cooking class there when she was about your age." I wonder if Bubbe forced her to go. Somehow, I kind of doubt it.

Bubbe's always saying how friendly Mom was as

a child. How she liked to talk with everyone, even adults. I think Dad was a little more like me. He says he always had a few good buddies, and they used to go fishing together because they lived near a canal. Fishing sounds quiet and relaxing. Too bad there isn't a fishing class at the community center.

"But dance! That's even more exciting," says Bubbe. "I bet you'll love it. I've been taking Zumba at my temple, you know. They have a morning class for sporty seniors." She chuckles.

"That's great." I feel like dirt. Bubbe thinks we have something else in common, besides our love for reading, chocolate-chip mandel bread, and extra-fluffy pillows.

"We'll have to trade moves next time I see you," Bubbe adds.

I'm doomed. I might as well come clean now. Gig's over before it even started.

"That would be fun." It's hard to sound enthusiastic.

"I'm starving! Let's make dinner," Mom interrupts.

Thanks for saving me, Mom. I say goodbye to Bubbe and hang up the phone. "What's for dinner?"

"It's no-fuss sandwich night."

"Okay." I open a cabinet door. "One can of tuna or two?"

"No tuna. The smell makes me nauseous."

I shut the cabinet door on eight cans of white tuna in two neat stacks. We've been making tuna since I was in kindergarten and Mom convinced me it was the lunch of champions. But she's laying pieces of turkey onto our whole wheat bread. By the time the baby's born, we'll be eating mush along with it.

Dad walks in while I'm setting the table. "How're you doing, *sheyne meydl*?"

I roll my eyes at the way he uses the Yiddish words that mean *pretty girl*. "Fine."

"Tell him about your summer class," Mom says as the three of us sit down at the table.

"I'm taking dance," I mumble.

"Dance? That's wonderful," Dad says.

"Yeah." Dad actually seems excited. I feel so bad lying.

Dad takes a big bite of his sandwich. A little mayo drips onto his shirt. "Who knows—this might be a new hobby for you, Sydney."

I hand him a paper towel. "Doubt it."

"Sydney, taking a class is not meant as a punishment," Mom says. "It will help you calm your nerves and reach your full potential."

Every time she mentions *potential*, I can tell she's thinking of the county spelling bee. "Mom, I know you think me skipping the spelling bee was a big deal, but I probably would've lost anyway."

And then I would've died of embarrassment—because what if I lost on a really simple word like *caustic* or *diagnostic*? All it takes is one word to get ejected. No second chances.

"What makes you think that? You won the school bee," Dad says.

"Yeah, but I was a disaster. My face turned red, and I could barely breathe, and Mr. Holly told me like a billion times to speak up."

"You were not a disaster. You were the winner," Mom says, using her outdoor voice.

I cover my ears. "Fluke."

Mom shakes her head. "Don't say that. You're a terrific speller, just like me."

"Maybe," I say. "But when Mr. Holly told me that the next step was the county competition, I freaked. I couldn't see myself on a stage at a school I'd never been to. That's why I told him I wouldn't be able to go."

It was kind of like in third grade when I was

supposed to step up from Brownies to Juniors. All I had to do was recite the Girl Scout pledge on the little stepping-over bridge. When Mom drove me there, I froze and couldn't even get out of the car. I told Mom I had a terrible stomachache, and she took me home. She finally caught on to me after I wolfed down dinner. She said I could've quit if I'd just told her I wanted to. But the truth is I liked my troop. I just didn't want to get up on that bridge.

"With any luck, this dance class will help you get past some of those fears," Mom says.

Ugh. The dance class.

I know Maggie thinks her plan of switching classes is a no-brainer, but my brain hurts just from thinking about it. So many things could go wrong.

Our parents could insist on signing us in on the first day.

We could know somebody in one of our classes who could blow our cover.

Maggie could have a change of heart and decide she really wants to take reading after all.

Okay, I admit that the third possibility is the least likely, but I still think this plan is risky. The last thing I want is to end up shaking my hips in front of a bunch of other kids.

## CHAPTER 4

The next day, after lunch, I walk over to Maggie's house.

Butter greets me at the door. I reach down to pet him. "You're so cute."

"Thanks." Maggie fluffs her hair.

"Oh, you too." I laugh. "Where's everyone else?"

"My mom's at the supermarket, and Jake is hanging out with a girl in the family room."

"Really? The same girl he's been texting all week?"

"Yes, that's her! You have to see her. She has the best hair."

"Well, I can't just barge into the family room and stare at her."

"True. I guess we need to come up with a reason to go in."

"My mom always says kill them with kindness!" I grab a pretzel from the open bag on the counter.

"We could put together a tray of snacks and offer them something to eat."

Maggie claps. "That's brilliant!"

"Thanks." I take a bow.

Maggie opens the kitchen pantry, and we grab some crackers to go with the pretzels. Her parents keep the shelves fully stocked because Jake eats enough for three.

I snag a big blue tray off the bottom shelf, and we arrange the snacks on it. We add some baby carrots and even find a creamy spread.

When we're done, we edge slowly into the family room. "Hi! What are you guys doing?" Maggie says.

"What does it look like?" Jake snaps. He's wearing a T-shirt that says *Butt Out* with a picture of a donkey's butt. I wonder what the girl thinks of that.

"Oh, is this your sister?" The girl sits up straight.

Maggie sets the tray down on the coffee table and holds out her hand. "Hi. I'm Maggie, Jake's amazing sister. Nice to meet you."

"I'm Olivia." The girl returns the shake. Maggie was right. She has long, shampoo-commercial shiny brown hair. She glances at me. "And who are you?"

"Sydney," I say softly.

"Cindy?" she asks.

"No, Sid-nee," Maggie corrects her.

"Okay. How old are you guys?" Olivia asks.

"Eleven," Maggie replies.

"Wow! You're so tall." She points at me.

I don't say anything. It's not a question.

"Sydney's like a giant." Jake laughs.

I still don't respond. Mostly because I don't know what to say. Besides, I've been called worse. A few months ago, we went out to dinner, and the restaurant host took one look at my new orange sneakers and burst out laughing. "Clown feet. What a funny sight," he said. Mom didn't hear him, and I was afraid to tell her. If she'd found out, she would've said something to the host and made an even bigger deal out of it. My mom has a powerful voice. Everyone in the restaurant would've heard. And then, for the rest of our meal, whenever someone walked by our table, they would've been sneaking peeks at my feet.

That was one of the first times I started hyperventilating. Mom and Dad thought I was allergic to something I'd eaten, but at that point, I'd only eaten the free breadsticks. Mom took me for allergy testing a few days later, and I came up negative for everything except mild sensitivities to dust mites, cockroaches, and kiwi. I really hope none of those things were in the breadsticks.

A squirrel races up a tree on the huge TV mounted on the wall. Jake and Olivia are actually watching Animal Planet. I wonder what Jake's buddies would think about that.

"We made you some snacks." Maggie slides the tray closer to them.

"Oh, carrots. I love carrots!" Olivia snatches one from the tray.

Jake crams a handful of pretzels into his mouth. "Okay, thanks. Now beat it."

"So ungrateful." Maggie scrunches up her face.

"Come on." I pull her away. I need to get out of here before Jake says something else embarrassing about me. But when we're a few steps away, I hear Olivia say, "What's up with the tall one? She hardly talks."

Ugh, I feel so stupid. I run up to Maggie's room as fast as I can.

"Don't worry about her," Maggie says when we're safely cocooned by her bright purple walls.

I know I shouldn't care what some random girl thinks about me, but I can't help it. "Why did she have to tell me I'm tall? Like I haven't noticed."

"Who knows? But you're lucky to be tall. Mom says I got my short genes from my grandmothers. They're both five feet."

"I don't feel lucky, though. My grandmas are both short too. See, I'm a freak of nature." I stretch out my legs and stare at my gigantic flippers.

"You are so not."

I check out my face in the mirror over Maggie's dresser. Light pink. I call that Phase 2, mostly only noticeable by me. There are five phases: normal, light pink, pink, dark pink, and bright red. Mrs. Leon, my school guidance counselor, made me identify them. At the time, I thought it was silly. But when she told me I'd get to miss PE, I sat right down and made the chart, complete with a color code.

"You look fine," Maggie insists.

"Okay." I pull away from the mirror. "Just checking to make sure I'm not bright red."

"At least it's summer, so a lot of people are red." She plops down into her saggy, old beanbag chair. "Plus, it's better than having orange skin from an overdose of carrots."

I snort. "Olivia doesn't have orange skin."

"She has an orange glow to her." Maggie throws her hands up in the air. "*I love carrots!*"

"Yeah, who says that?"

"But her hair *is* great, right? If I had hair like that, guys at school would notice me for sure." Maggie gets up and walks over to the long mirror on her closet door. She puckers her lips and blows a kiss.

"You want guys at school to notice you?" I ask.

"Well, there must be at least some cute guys at Coral Rock Middle next year."

"I'm not holding my breath." I push Maggie's heap of stuffed animals aside so I have more room to spread out on the floor.

"Maybe I should straighten my hair." Maggie pulls one of her curls straight.

"No way. Your hair looks great as it is."

"Maybe the secret is in the carrots."

I laugh. "I wonder what shampoo she uses." I think of all those shampoo commercials where the girl swishes her hair back and forth.

"I'll give her a sniff next time," says Maggie with a laugh.

When we go back downstairs to grab some water, Olivia and Jake are at the front door.

"Do you really have to leave?" he whines.

"I can't miss orientation. Classes start tomorrow."

"I can't believe you're going to be working all

day. What am I going to do without you?"

"When did he get so desperate?" I whisper to Maggie.

"I know! It's pathetic," Maggie says.

"You can play Xbox all day." Olivia laughs. "Unless you want to sign up for a class at the community center."

Community center?

Oh, crud.

"I'm taking a class there," Maggie blurts out.

No! What is she thinking? We can't draw attention to ourselves.

Oliva breaks free from Jake's embrace. "Really? Which class?"

"Dance combo."

"Cool! I'm working at the front desk," Olivia says.

I stomp on Maggie's foot.

"Ouch." She winces. "I mean, reading. I'm taking a reading class. Sydney's taking dance."

"Sydney in a dance class!" Jake laughs. "I've got to see that!"

I glare at Maggie.

"Don't worry! I've got a plan," she whispers.

"A plan to kill me," I mumble. Things have gone from worse to worse than worse.

## CHAPTER 5

"Almost ready?" Mom calls up to my room on Monday morning.

"Yes." Even though I'm nervous about being caught and thrown into community center jail, I try to act normal. Every time I want to back out—which is basically every other second—I think about the phone I want to get with the cool case that changes color. It's called a color mood case. And right now, my mood is red hot.

"Let's go." Mom holds up her keys. The tiny clay snail I made her in art class swings back and forth on her keychain. I wish I were a snail right about now and could hide in my shell.

"Are you sure about those clothes?" she asks me.

I'm wearing jean shorts, a plain blue T-shirt, and sneakers—not the dancewear Mom bought me over the weekend. Bicycle shorts and bright workout shirts with geometric shapes are just not my thing. And I don't want the other students in the reading class to be blinded by my outfit. "I think this will be fine for the first day," I say.

In the car, Mom listens to her audiobook about raising a child in a technology-obsessed society, and I'm glued to the family iPad. I don't tell her I'm playing Spelling Wiz because if I did, she'd probably make me sign up for the spelling club the first day of sixth grade.

After the school bee, I had nightmares for a couple of weeks. In my dreams, huge letters chased me through the hallways, and all the kids were laughing. I know it sounds silly, but when I was stuck inside the dream and couldn't get out, it was very scary.

I mean, if I had won the county spelling bee, which I totally wouldn't have, it wouldn't have made me popular or anything. Mr. Holly sent Mitchell Bucket in my place. He came in third. He's not cool. He chews his shoelaces. I didn't think that was possible until I saw him and his bony knees in action. He lost on the word *cacti*. A bunch of kids started calling him Cacti King after that. Mitchell thought it was funny. I did not. Luckily, I know how to spell *cacti*, *c-a-c-t-i*.

Mom pulls up to the community center, and I'm surprised to see it's been freshly painted a minty cream. Not my favorite color for a building, but much better than the peeling peach that was on it the last time we came here.

"Hey, Mom, you can just drop me off." I unclip my seat belt.

"Are you sure?"

"Yeah, totally." I open the door before she can change her mind.

She glances at the nearly full parking lot. "Okay. I'll see you at noon." She kisses me on the forehead. "Have a great time!"

Wow, that was easy. "I'll try."

Here goes nothing. I gulp in a breath of fresh air before I walk through the double doors. There's already a line to check in. A few parents are waiting with their kids, but the rest are on their own. I look around for Maggie. She'll be coming straight from her orthodontist appointment, so we couldn't carpool.

A couple of teen girls are working at the front desk. One is definitely Olivia.

Ugh, how do I make sure she's not the one to check me in? For now, I'm staying out of her view, but that's not going to last forever. It's kind of hard to hide when you're tall.

I bite the inside of my lip. Maggie had better get here soon. I have a bad feeling about this whole thing. Maybe neither of us should go to class. We could hide out in the field behind the community center and reappear for pickup each day. Too bad it's so hot outside that you can melt crayons on the sidewalk.

I'm three people away from the front of the line when I spot Maggie coming through the front door. Finally!

"Over here!" I loud-whisper.

She spots me and runs over, practically screaming my name.

"Shh!" I put my finger over my lips. "Remember, we're trying to be low key."

"Don't worry about it. I told you, I've got a plan."

"That's what I'm worried about," I groan.

"Frankelstein, when have I let you down?"

"Do I really have to tell you now?"

"Next," Olivia calls.

Maggie waltzes right up to her. "How's it going, Olivia? Jake is out front. He wants to say a quick hi."

"Now?" She tucks her hair behind her ears.

"Trust me. It's important." Maggie winks at her.

Olivia turns to the girl next to her and says she'll be right back. She speed walks out of the building.

Man, I can't believe Maggie. She's overflowing with guts.

She turns to the other girl at the desk. "I'm Sydney A . . ."

I quickly slap her arm. She'd better not say my middle name! Maggie is the only person outside my family who knows it, and I'm keeping it that way.

"Sydney Frankel," she says. "In the dance combo class."

"Oh, you're going to love it!" the check-in girl says. "My mom teaches it. It's in Room 10, down the hall to the left."

What is wrong with this place? Everybody knows everybody. I can't hide anywhere.

The girl checks something off a list and looks at me. "And you?"

"Maggie." The big liar.

She snaps her gum. "Last name?"

"Stein. In the reading class."

"Gotcha. You're all set. Room 8."

I see Olivia running back inside, her ponytail flapping back and forth.

I elbow Maggie.

"Let's get out of here!" Maggie takes off before I can even respond.

I run after her. "Olivia's going to be so mad at Jake."

"I know." Maggie laughs. "But we're in!"

I look up at the classroom numbers in front of us. Dance is a couple of doors down from reading.

"We've got this!" Maggie holds her hand up and we high-five. "Frankelstein power!"

I hope we have enough Frankelstein power to make it through the whole summer.

# CHAPTER 6

A boy rushes past me toward Room 8. He nearly bumps into me. I take a step back to steady myself.

"Oh, sorry, I didn't see you there." He motions for me to enter first. "I'm such a klutz."

Didn't see me? No one ever says that. "It's okay," I say.

I have no choice now but to enter the classroom. I take a deep breath and walk inside. The teacher is sitting at the big desk against the back wall. She's wearing a navy dress with a lot of buttons, and she looks as if she has a very good iron at home. Not even one wrinkle on her dress.

"Welcome!" she says. "Have a seat, and we'll get started in a minute."

I slink into a desk. The klutzy kid sits next to me.

A few seconds later, three other kids stroll in, two with their moms and one alone. The girl with long blonde hair blows a bubble with her gum, and her mom tells her to throw it away. The other girl is really small and doesn't say a word. The boy has a huge grin on his face. I don't know what he could possibly be so happy about.

At exactly eleven, the teacher introduces herself as Mrs. Wrigley. Two more kids walk in, and once they've taken their seats, she starts to take attendance.

"Ollie Moore."

"Here," shouts the klutzy kid.

"Margaret Stein."

Silence.

"Margaret Stein?" She raises her voice, looking around.

"Oh, sorry," I say. "I spaced out."

Maggie hates to be called Margaret. The only person who does that is the rabbi at our temple. And of course, she's never going to correct *him*.

But should I say something? I don't want to call more attention to myself. But Mrs. Wrigley is already moving on to the next person. "Hailey Townsend."

"Yep." The blonde girl raises her hand.

Well, I guess I'm Margaret.

I look around the room. There are only six other students here. I didn't expect this class to be packed, but I thought we'd at least have a few more people. How am I going to hide in a class of seven kids?

Mrs. Wrigley hands out folders and tells us to bring them to every class. They're filled with paper for taking notes and journaling. Why so much writing for a reading class? This is sounding more and more like summer school.

I expected her to pass out a stack of books. Then we could all just dive in and discuss what we're reading.

Mrs. Wrigley passes out colored pencils to everyone. "Take a piece of paper from your folder and draw a picture of yourself and your family. When you're done, you'll each tell your classmates a little about your drawing." Correction: This is sounding more and more like preschool.

"I thought this was a reading class," says the redheaded boy in back, the only kid wearing long sleeves.

Exactly.

"It sure is, Calvin. But to be solid readers, we have to know our own stories. There are many components to reading."

Could've fooled me. I always thought the steps were pretty simple.

Open the book.

Read.

Close the book.

Mom did warn me that this is reading *improvement* class, though. I guess most of these kids probably aren't voracious readers like I am.

The blonde girl, Hailey, raises her hand. "But I have three sisters and a brother and two dogs and a goldfish. Drawing all of them is going to take forever."

Show-off.

"Why don't you just draw the humans, Hailey?" Mrs. Wrigley suggests.

"Fine." Hailey draws a huge circle in the middle of the paper. "I'll start with myself."

I stare at the blank sheet of paper in front of me. I don't know if I should draw my family or Maggie's family. This is confusing. If I draw my family, it'll be kind of boring. Maggie at least has her brother.

I guess I'll stick with my family, since I don't really want to have to talk about Jake. If anyone asks me personal questions about him, it'll be a disaster. All I can say is he eats a lot and yells at the TV during football games.

I sketch Dad first. I give him some extra hair

like he always wants and a curlicue mustache because it makes me laugh. Mom's next, wearing the green maternity shirt that she said she saved from when she was pregnant with me. I flip up her long brown hair at the ends. After that, I draw myself. I give myself a colorful shirt because I know that's what Mom wants me to wear. My hair's the same as Mom's except a little shorter. Finally, I draw a kidney bean floating in front of Mom's stomach. Mom told me the baby is the size of a kidney bean. I add a tuft of hair on top, some eyes, and stick arms and legs.

Behind me, Calvin stands up and peers over my shoulder. "That looks like poop."

I stare at the picture. He's right. "The poop emoji," I say.

He laughs. I feel my face redden.

"It's actually the baby my mom is about to have," I blurt out. "It's just a bean right now."

This gets Ollie's attention. "A bean?" he echoes.

Ugh. Why didn't I just keep quiet? "A kidney bean." I sink lower into my seat, hoping a hole will open up in the linoleum floor and suck me down.

"That's cool," says Ollie. "I wish I had a brother or a sister."

I don't know what to say to that. Calvin goes

back to his drawing, leaving Ollie and me to stare at each other.

"I'm Ollie," he says.

"I know." I nod.

"Right. There's only seven of us in here."

"Yup. Nowhere to hide."

"Not even at home." Ollie folds his arms and leans back in his chair. "Being an only child is hard sometimes."

"I'm used to it. Do you have any pets?"

"Yeah—a pet turtle, Mr. Toad."

"Cool!" I'd love to have a pet, especially a dog. Dad's allergic to them, though, and I think Mom's secretly glad, because she's not a huge fan of the vacuum. I love Maggie's dog, but he's constantly shedding all over her furniture and carpet.

"Mr. Toad is great," Ollie says. "But he doesn't stop my parents from breathing down my neck. I bet it would be different if we had a baby. I could eat whatever I wanted and have way more Xbox time." He takes a purple pencil and fills in the sky on his paper.

"Guess you have a point," I say. "My parents are kind of like that too."

Maybe they want me to be more independent

so they can have extra time with the adorable little baby. Who wants to drive a too-tall, whiny, red-faced middle schooler around when you can play peekaboo with a smiling cutie?

After we're done with our masterpieces, we're supposed to stand up at our desks and share them. I'm already starting to hyperventilate. It's so annoying. I wish I had more control over it. When teachers tell me to speak up, I speak up. When Mom tells me to read with more enthusiasm, I try to sound all chirpy, but it's hard to keep my breathing normal.

I should have some water. It's important for me to be properly hydrated before I start speaking, or my throat dries up and nothing comes out. I pick up my water bottle and start drinking and drinking.

Ollie leans over. "Geez, you're really thirsty."

It's not actually a question, so I just nod and finish the bottle.

"Do you need another one?" He pulls a water bottle out of his backpack.

"No, thanks. I'm good."

"Want some of this?" He takes out a small tube of hand lotion. Wow, this guy is more prepared than my bubbe and her kitchen-sink purse, as Zayde calls it.

"It's calming lotion with a hint of lavender," he adds.

"Sure. Thanks." I squeeze a little bit into my hands and rub it in. Why didn't I think of this before? It could've gotten me out of a lot of bad situations. I close my eyes for a second. "I feel calmer already."

"You're weird." He laughs.

"I know."

Mrs. Wrigley asks a girl named Sara to say a few words about her picture. She has a flat, toneless voice that reminds me of a robot. "I . . . have . . . one . . . broth . . . er. He . . . is . . . four . . . teen."

I wonder if he sounds like a robot too.

Breathe in. Breathe out. It's Hailey's turn next. Then it'll be Ollie, then me. Gulp.

Hailey's one bubbly girl. She goes into detail about all her siblings and then moves on to her pets. We even learn which brand of cereal they each like best. When Mrs. Wrigley is about to thank her and go to the next person, Hailey says, "Wait! You're not going to believe this, but my mom is pregnant with twins! I'm not supposed to tell anyone until after the first trimester, but I couldn't keep it from you guys."

Great—way to squash my kidney bean surprise.

Now what am I going to say? I have a mom, dad, no pets, blah, blah, boring, snoring!

Mrs. Wrigley smiles at Hailey. "You must be excited."

Hailey beams, and my stomach sinks to my knees.

Ollie stands up and takes his time talking, kind of like my zayde. He says his turtle is like his brother. Calvin and Hailey laugh at that.

"And now we're going to hear from Margaret," Mrs. Wrigley says. She's standing inches from my desk. A little personal space would be nice.

I scoot my chair back a smidgen. I think she gets the picture, because she takes a step back too.

Mrs. Wrigley nods. I nod back. She has a nice smile with super-white teeth. I bet people tell her that a lot.

"When is Margaret going to talk?" Hailey asks.

Mrs. Wrigley ignores her but nods at me again. My face feels warm, my throat's dry, and I have a huge urge to run out of the room. Here goes nothing.

I take a deep breath. "I have no pets. I'm an only child. Well, not for long. My mom's having a baby in October."

"You're a singleton?" Hailey asks.

"You mean one?" I shrug.

"Duh!" says Calvin.

"More and more families are deciding to have just one child," says a girl named Alice whose face is half covered by long bangs. "There's been a big shift in the last few decades."

Mrs. Wrigley smiles at her. "Good point, Alice. So it's interesting that in this class, there are three new babies on the way." She rubs her hands together. "Exciting times."

"Do you have any kids?" Calvin shouts at her.

"Yes, I have three," Mrs. Wrigley answers. "My youngest is going to be a junior in college this year."

"Wow, you don't seem that old," Calvin says, extra loud again.

"Thanks." She chuckles.

"People are living longer and longer these days," says Alice. "The average global life expectancy is now 72.6 years."

Mrs. Wrigley nods and then tells us about her kids. I'm happy to listen because that means we have officially moved the spotlight off me and over to her. Maybe I should thank Calvin and his loud interruptions.

There's one girl who hasn't spoken at all. Her name's Mary, and she sits way over on the left side of the room. She's tiny and wears glasses like Ollie and I do. When it's her turn, Mrs. Wrigley squeezes through the desks and stands next to her. Mary points to some words on her paper, and Mrs. Wrigley reads them to us. Turns out Mary has two older brothers, three cats, and a goldfish. She lived in China for two years and Hawaii for three. Even without talking, Mary manages to make her life sound more exciting than mine!

"And that's about all the time we have today." Mrs. Wrigley gestures to the clock on the wall. "But our journey together has just begun. I'm going to send you home with an assignment. Fill it out, and we'll share next class."

"Homework?" Calvin groans loudly. He sounds like a grizzly bear. I have to hold in my laughter.

"What does this have to do with reading?" Ollie grumbles.

I nod at him, since I was thinking the same thing.

"This will help me decide what types of stories we'll be tackling in this class. I like to get to know my students first. Don't worry—it's a fun assignment." Mrs. Wrigley gives us each a handout. It says, *Reading Express Personal Inventory: Get to Know Yourself Better.* I already know me, and I know I don't like talking about myself, especially when I'm supposed to be someone I'm not.

I think Mrs. Wrigley can see the worry lines on my face, because she leans over my desk and whispers, "Trust me—this exercise is very helpful. You'll be surprised what you'll learn."

Yeah. I've already learned that my teacher and I have very different definitions of fun.

## CHAPTER 7

After class, Maggie's waiting for me right by the front door of the community center—and so is Mom. Argh, why did she get out of the car?

"How was it?" Mom asks me. "Not too bad?"

If I say it *was* bad, she'll want more info. "No, it was fine."

"Excellent." She looks me up and down. "But you don't look sweaty at all."

"Uh, that's because we did a bunch of icebreakers today." Which is technically not a lie. I just happened to do them in another classroom without any loud music.

Mom smiles. "See? You're adjusting already."

If only she knew that not only did I have to go to a class, but I also had to pretend to be my best friend. I've been Sydney for eleven years—it's hard to be someone else at this point in my life.

"Is your teacher still there?" Mom asks. "I'd like to introduce myself."

"Why, Mom? It's not *your* class!" I grab her arm. "Let's go home."

"Aw, come on, Sydney . . ."

"Shh." I look around to make sure no one heard her say my name. I don't want her to blow my cover this early.

"What's going on with you?" Mom asks. "I'll just pop in for a minute."

Geez, what part of *no* does she not get? We're one step away from having our whole plan fall apart. I glance at Maggie, but she looks as panicked as I feel.

"Mom, it would be really embarrassing. None of the other parents are going in." I bite the inside of my lip. "Can we please just leave? I'm starving."

Mom pats her stomach. "Me too. Okay, I'll talk to your teacher another time."

I hold my breath all the way to the car. That was such a close call.

\* \* \*

Back home, as soon as I'm done with lunch, I plan to spend the rest of the day stretched out on the family room couch, watching a Disney Channel movie marathon and enjoying the AC. I'm in the kitchen, waiting for my bag of popcorn in the microwave, when Mom comes in. Her stomach looks a bit bulgier.

"Is the baby still the size of a kidney bean?" I ask.

"Oh, no." Mom looks around the kitchen for a second and picks up a banana from the fruit bowl. "It's almost as big as this now."

"Really?" I'm not sure if class would've been more or less embarrassing if I had drawn a banana coming out of my mom.

"The baby's growing fast." Mom smiles. "But not as fast as you! Soon you'll be taller than I am."

"Ugh, I know." Why'd she have to remind me? Mom's five feet nine inches tall, and Dr. Heller said I'll probably be a couple of inches taller than that. In fact, what she said was, "You'll be knocking on six feet's door and turning heads." I know she meant that as a compliment, but it's hard to stay in the shadows when you're the one who creates them.

"Anyway," Mom says, opening the fridge, "I'm going to the Pendlers' house now."

"That's nice," I say as I watch the bag of popcorn expand. Bubbe told me that you're not supposed to watch the microwave because you could go cross-eyed, so I only glance out of the corner of my eye.

"I'd like you to come with me, Sydney."

Now she has my full attention. "Why?"

"To welcome Warren and Mark and their mom back to the neighborhood, that's why. It's been three years since we last saw them! I baked them a kugel."

I look at the sweet cheese noodle dish she's just taken out of the fridge. I should've known. It's my favorite, and Mom usually only makes it for Jewish holidays.

"Oh." *Pop. Pop. Pop.* I hope the popcorn doesn't burn. "I thought you baked that for us."

"No, we're having spaghetti for dinner."

The microwave beeps, and I pull the bag out, watching the steam escape. "That's not fair. If they don't like the kugel, can we keep it?"

"Everyone likes kugel."

"Well, maybe they're allergic to cheese."

"The whole family?"

"Could be. I've seen TV shows like that." I shove a few kernels of popcorn into my mouth.

"Sydney, are you trying to tell me people don't like my kugel?"

Mom's voice wobbles a little. Is she crying? No, she can't be. What has this baby done to her?

"No, Mom! People love your kugel! Especially me." I put down the popcorn bag and give her a big hug. "Well, it's not like I took a survey or anything, but *I* love your kugel." And it sure smells good right about now. "It's just that Warren's kind of weird, and I wouldn't have anything to talk to him about, okay?"

Warren is my age. His brother, Mark, is way older, so I know Mom will expect me to focus my friendliness on Warren.

She pulls away from my hug. "He's a lovely boy. I'm sure you'll find plenty in common to chat about."

"Mom, the last time I saw him, he blew his nose with his sleeve."

"So?"

"So that's gross." I lick the popcorn salt off my fingers. Mom shakes her head at me. Busted, I grab a napkin. "Plus, he wears sweatbands and keeps his socks pulled up all the way."

Mom puts her hands on her hips. "Now, come on. Since when is that a crime? It's not very kind to judge people based on how they dress."

We both look over at the word of the day board. It says *remorse*. Oh, that was planned.

"Fine, I'll go with you." I don't want to be stuck with a whole day of guilt.

We walk up the street to the Pendlers' house. Usually there are at least a couple of neighbors out. But not today. Maybe that's a sign. Or it could be the weather. It's taken a whole two seconds for the sweat to pool up on my forehead. Miami in June is like Mercury.

Mom stops to adjust the tinfoil covering the kugel. "You don't have to be afraid of Mrs. Pendler, Sydney."

"Why are you saying that?" I ask, even though I know the answer.

"Mr. Smith," Mom says gently. "Another reason why learning to speak up is so important for you."

I scuff my sneaker on the pavement. That was over a year ago, but Mom keeps bringing it up. Our neighbor Jenny Smith borrowed my new scooter and never brought it back. Mom told me to go to her house and get it. But I didn't want to ring the doorbell because I was afraid of her dad. He has a full beard and looks like a WWE wrestler. Mom said there was nothing to be afraid of. She's known him forever. I didn't go over. Instead, I waited three whole days until Maggie saw Jenny using the scooter and brought it back to me. Those were three long, scooterless days.

We wind up the stone walkway to the green house with yellow shutters. I haven't been to this house in a while. Two pilots were renting it after the Pendlers moved away, and they were hardly ever home. Mom rings the doorbell. I stand directly behind her and cringe. What are Warren and I going to talk about? Boogers? Sweatbands? More boogers?

Nobody comes. Mom shifts the kugel from her right hip to her left. She sighs.

Oh, no! She's not supposed to be lifting heavy things. "Want me to hold it?" I ask.

"No, no, thanks. I'm fine."

Just when I'm about to tell Mom to leave the food on the front step and make a run for it, the door swings open with a bash.

"Hello, Madeline! Good to see you." Mrs. Pendler tilts her head toward me. "Sydney, is that you?"

I squeak out a "Yes."

"You look so grown up. And so tall! Are you excited for the baby?" Her cheeks are rosy, kind of like mine were in class yesterday.

"Oh, yeah."

"I remember when Warren was a baby. Seems like just yesterday," she says.

I picture a baby with snot all over his face, wearing a sweatband. I know all babies are supposed to be cute, but I bet he wasn't.

"Come in, come in." Mrs. Pendler takes the kugel from Mom. "That smells delicious."

"It's a kugel," Mom says.

"Thank you! I'm sure we'll gobble it up right away," Mrs. Pendler says as we follow her into the house. My eyes try to adjust to the red kitchen, brighter than Jupiter.

"The kitchen is lovely," Mom says.

"Do you like it?" Mrs. Pendler asks. "I wanted to do something different. Our kitchen in Chicago was so drab."

"I like those." I point to the whole row of different-colored jars set up on the counter.

"Thanks. Warren helped me pick them out. You know, it'll be so nice for you two to be neighbors again." She smiles.

I picture me and Stinky Sweatband Boy eating dinner together, watching TV, dusting the colored jars. My stomach swirls. How could Mom do this to me?

"I was thinking about signing him up for debate

team at the middle school. Are you interested? It's a new program for the fall. They have a retired coach coming from Chicago. Imagine that—we leave Chicago to get a coach from Chicago!"

"Ahh . . ." I glance over at Mom, hoping she'll save me from answering.

"Don't worry. You have plenty of time to think about it," Mrs. Pendler says.

I need less than a nanosecond to think about that. There aren't enough *N*s and *O*s in the world to cover my answer. In debate, you get assigned topics and have to talk about them. That's worse than any spelling bee ever.

"Mark has been doing debate for three years," Mrs. Pendler goes on. "It's been great for him. He'll be a high school junior in the fall."

"Hey, Mom." A tall boy with spiky brown hair comes bounding in from the garage. He nods at Mom and me. "Oh, hi."

"Warren, you remember Sydney, don't you?" Mrs. Pendler waves her arm at me, and all her bracelets jingle as if she's on a holiday float.

Warren? I do a double take. He's not wearing anything across his forehead. His T-shirt looks booger-free. This must be another Warren.

"Yeah, hi. What's up?" He leans on the other end of the counter.

"Um, nothing." Could I be any more boring? But seriously, he looks completely different from the old Warren. I think I need to move to Chicago too.

Mrs. Pendler boils a cup of tea for Mom and sets out a plate of chocolate chip cookies for us.

Warren takes a stack of three and gobbles them up. Okay, that part hasn't changed. But he actually uses a napkin and wipes his face afterward. Maybe his mom sent him to one of those cotillion classes where they teach you how to have proper manners.

"What are you doing this summer?" Warren asks me.

"Nothing much."

"You're taking a dance class," Mom butts in. My face turns the color of the kitchen walls in a split second. She'd better not say anything else.

"How fun." Mrs. Pendler sips her tea.

"It wasn't my idea," I say. "I was forced to pick something."

"She'll thank me for it later," Mom says. "It's actually dance combo. She'll be learning different types."

"Sounds fun! Warren's going to basketball camp,

and he's playing on the YMCA's summer league. Do you play?" Mrs. Pendler asks me.

I shake my head. Mom glares at me. I don't know why she's annoyed. It was a yes or no question.

"With your height, you'd be a good center," Mrs. Pendler says.

"It's not only about how tall you are," Warren interrupts.

"I'm just saying that Sydney might like to play. She could be dunking in no time." Mrs. Pendler winks at me.

Dunking? Really? Did she take the embarrassing-mom oath too?

Warren rolls his eyes at her.

Mrs. Pendler holds up the cookie plate. Warren grabs another one, but Mom and I say, "No, thanks."

"Well, we should leave you to finish unpacking." Mom gets up from the table.

Finally, she's received my telepathic SOS message: Evacuate the premises NOW, before my faces goes polka dot or she says anything else to embarrass me.

I look over at Warren. It's hard to believe he's the same boy who used to ride his bike up and down the street, trying and failing to pop wheelies.

"See you around," I say.

"Yeah. Good luck with your dance class." He throws me a small wave and disappears back into the garage. I wonder what he's doing in there. Maybe that's where he morphs back into his old self.

We say goodbye to Mrs. Pendler and walk back home.

When we reach our front door, Mom asks. "Well, do you still hate Warren?"

"I never said I hated him. But why did you tell him about my stupid class?"

"I didn't think it was a big deal. I thought dance was cool."

"Taking a summer class is not cool, Mom. I'm sure he thinks I'm weird now."

"So you do care." Mom smiles.

Ugh, parents. What happened to their brains?

## CHAPTER 8

When I get inside, I snatch the phone and run up to my room to call Maggie. I can hardly dial her number fast enough. "Maggie, you're not going to believe this, but Warren Pendler is normal now." I sit down on my bed and kick off my shoes.

"For real?" she says. "How do you know?"

"Remember how I told you he moved back to our street? My mom made us bring him a kugel today."

"No way. Did he flick a booger at you?"

"Nope, and he wasn't wearing his socks pulled up high, and he didn't have a sweatband on." I'm pacing back and forth on my fluffy blue carpet. Why am I pacing?

"Wow. Are you sure it was the same guy?"

"Of course! How many Warren Pendlers are there?"

"Hmm." She pauses for a second. "Maybe his

parents traded him in for a better model."

"I thought about that, but he has that scar on his eyebrow from the wheelie accident in second grade."

"Does he still have the bowl haircut?"

"Oh, no, it's kind of spiky now. He's tall too. And I think he even has some muscles."

All of a sudden, I hear a lot of banging around on the other end.

"What are you doing, Maggie?"

"Just looking for something to bring to the Pendlers so I can see Warren."

"Are you serious?" I take out my box of nail polishes and arrange the bottles in rainbow order. Everything is here except yellow.

"Yeah . . . Do you think a bag of Goldfish would be okay? Or a jar of organic strawberry mango jam, but it's been opened?"

"Why don't you just go ring the doorbell and say hello?" I shake the red bottle. The polish inside looks kind of crusty.

"Yeah, that's a good idea. Want to come with?"

"Uh, thanks, but no. I was just there." I sit down on the carpet and pull off my socks. I stare at my bare feet.

"Come on. I'd do it for you," she says, all sugary sweet.

I tuck the phone under my left ear and paint my big toe red. "True. You would." I'm afraid of getting all red-faced and tongue-tied, but Maggie's not going to embarrass me like Mom did. "Okay, come get me in half an hour."

She squeals before hanging up.

I think of the colored jars in Warren's kitchen. I paint my next nail blue. My nails are five different colors by the time I hear Maggie knocking on the front door. I hobble-run downstairs to let her in, trying not to ruin the still-drying paint job.

"Looks nice," Maggie says as I wiggle my toes. "You went all out."

"Just needed something to do while I waited for you."

Maggie tugs my hand. "Well, let's go. We have to hurry."

"Why?" I ask.

"Warren might change back into his old self before we get there!"

"You're one wacky best friend," I say.

"Hey, I'm only one half of Frankelstein." She jabs me with her elbow.

I jab her right back. "Two halves make a whole."

I slip on a pair of flip-flops and yell goodbye to Mom. Maggie's halfway down my driveway before I can even shut the front door.

"We are cool." She starts skipping. She lightly taps the Johnsons' ceramic dolphin-head mailbox and dodges between two gigantic palm trees.

"We're super cool!" I skip to catch up with her.

"No, we are super-duper cool!" Maggie shouts.

"Shh." I hold a finger over my mouth. "We don't want anyone to hear."

"We're super-duper, pooper-scooper cool!" she shouts even more loudly.

"Hey." A head pops out from behind a tree.

My mouth drops. "Hi, Warren." So much for Maggie being less embarrassing than Mom.

Maggie's eyes practically pop out of her head like she's a cartoon character. "You're Warren?"

"Don't you remember me?" he asks.

She looks him up and down. "Yeah, but you're a lot . . ."

"Taller," I butt in so she doesn't make an even bigger fool of herself.

"Did you hear what I said a minute ago?" Maggie asks.

Or see us skipping up the street like toddlers?

He squints and lowers his baseball cap. "Something about a super scooper?"

"Right." I kick the huge coconut lying on the sidewalk. It rolls into the street. If I keep my head low, maybe Warren won't see my red face. "It's . . . an ice cream place."

"Sorry, what did you say?" he asks.

"She said it's an ice cream place, and we want to go there because it's really, really hot." Maggie fans herself with her hand.

Warren looks at me, then Maggie. "So where is this Scooper place? I've never heard of it."

"It's, uh, kind of out of business," Maggie says.

I step on her foot. Why did she have to say that?

"Okay, then," Warren says.

I wish I had a baseball cap like Warren's to hide under.

"Are you okay?" he asks me. "You look kind of flushed."

My face instantly shoots up to Phase 5, code red. I just nod.

"And you don't talk much," he adds.

I hate when people say that. It's not as if that's going to make me talk more.

Maggie steps in for me. "She's nursing a sunburn that causes her voice to go in and out like a bad cell phone connection."

"Oh, that's rough. Try aloe. My mom loves that stuff," Warren suggests.

I nod again, only proving his point that I don't talk much.

"Okay, I've got to run," Warren says, shooting us a wave. "We're going out to dinner."

I *knew* they weren't going to eat Mom's kugel tonight. So unfair.

Maggie says goodbye, but I just stand there like a doofus. She even has to nudge me to turn around and head back to my house.

"My voice goes in and out like a bad cell connection?" I crack up.

"Hey, don't I get points for quick thinking?" Maggie laughs too.

It takes me a second to refocus. To deblush. "Sure, I guess. But he probably thinks we're dorks."

"True." Maggie sighs. "He's never going to want to hang out with us now."

"Who wants to hang out with him anyway?" I walk right into a palm frond hanging over our driveway.

I turn around and see Maggie staring into space.

"Earth to Maggie. I *said*, 'Who wants to hang out with him anyway?'"

"Me." She smiles.

Oh, brother. Maggie is crushing on Warren. This is going to be one long summer.

# CHAPTER 9

Homework in June is just plain cruel. And we have to write down information about ourselves. Double cruel. I never know what to say. The first question asks what my favorite food is, but I don't have one favorite. For instance, if I said hamburger, I would want some fries with that. If I said salmon, I would need to write a disclaimer because Maggie's allergic, so I never have it when she's over. Or I guess, as far as my reading class knows, *I'm* allergic? This whole being-Maggie thing keeps tripping me up.

"What are you working so hard at?" Mom peeks over my shoulder at the kitchen table.

I cover the top of the paper with my hand so she won't see *Reading Express* printed there. Luckily, I've already taken the precaution of covering my class folder with ballet stickers. "A questionnaire about ourselves."

"Strange activity for a dance class."

*Strange activity for a reading class too*, I want to say. "The teacher wants to get to know us."

"Oh, that's nice. Hold on . . ."

I tense up. Is she getting suspicious?

"An apple?" she says, reading off the sheet. "Your favorite food is really an apple? I would've guessed french fries or pizza."

Whew. "No, it's more complicated than that." I explain my theory to her. "An apple is something you can have whenever, anytime of the day, so it's more practical."

She looks at me strangely. "And your favorite color is aquamarine?"

"Yes, because it combines two colors, green and blue. So you're less likely to get sick of it."

But really, my favorite color is green, and Maggie's is blue, and since I'm basically half me and half Maggie for the summer, aquamarine is the only color that makes sense.

I move on to the next question: best friend. Well, that's a no-brainer. I start to write a big *M* for Maggie until I remember that I have to write *Sydney*. I cover that question with my elbow so Mom won't see it. It's getting harder and harder to write with everything that I have to cover. I guess my long arms actually do come in handy sometimes.

I'm sailing along until I get to favorite hobby. Saying *reading* sounds boring. I like drawing, but I also like bike riding and swimming. I write down bike riding, because that's something Mom and I do together. Except now she's taking a break until the Kidney Bean/Banana is born. She says we can start riding together again after that, but I'm not so sure. I've heard that babies are a lot of work for parents and take up most of their time.

I picture the little squirt waking up in the middle of the night, crying its eyes out. I'm going to have to keep my door closed if I want to get any rest. And I've heard sixth grade is hard. What if I need help with my homework? How is Mom going to test me on vocabulary or help me prep for a dreaded presentation when the baby's screaming at the top of its lungs?

I look up at Mom, who's writing the new word of the day on the whiteboard.

"*Stifle?*" I wrinkle my nose. "What's that?"

Mom changes pen colors to write the definition. "When someone is unable to breathe properly. The feeling of being suffocated." Mom pops the marker cap back on and adds, "It can also be when someone is overwhelmed or feels a lack of freedom."

I think for a moment. "Sometimes I feel like that."

"Really?" Mom's eyes bug out.

Oh, no. Now I'm in trouble. I don't want to say anything about the baby because it will make her lip quiver and her eyes get all teary. So I pick the next best thing. "Like when I want to tell someone something, but I can't."

Mom stares at me. "For example?"

I shuffle my foot back and forth. "Well, remember how I had to wait until you were three months pregnant before I could tell anyone?"

"Aw, that's so sweet."

I feel a twinge of guilt. Okay, a big slice of guilt.

"Oh, wow." Mom looks down.

"What is it?"

"The baby." She touches her stomach.

"Is it okay?"

"Yes. I just felt it kick!"

"Really?" I picture a banana in a karate suit doing a *hi-YA*.

"Whoa, there it goes again. Come over and feel."

I get up from the table and put my hand lightly on her stomach. I can't believe how much it sticks out, and it's so hard. "I don't feel anything."

"Give it a minute," Mom says.

I move my hand slowly up and down. I watch the microwave clock change. Still nothing. I pull my hand away. "I guess the baby doesn't like me."

Mom leans over and pulls me closer. "Now, that's not true. Just you wait—when the baby is old enough to crawl, you'll have a little sibling chasing you all around the house."

"Seriously?"

"I'm certain. You'll be a fantastic big sister."

I fold my arms across my chest. "Maybe, but I'm not changing diapers."

"Who do you think changed *your* diapers?"

"I thought I was a super kid who was potty-trained from birth."

Mom laughs. "Quite the opposite—you were one messy pooper."

"Gross. I'm definitely not putting that on my questionnaire. I hope you don't tell anyone that. Ever."

"Your secret is safe with me." Mom pretends to zip her lips.

"Geez, I feel so protected."

Dad walks in. "Good evening, ladies. What are we chatting about?"

"Sydney's dirty diapers," Mom says.

"Mom!" I shout.

"I thought you were potty-trained." Dad laughs.

"What's wrong with you two? I'm going upstairs." I march off.

"Just joking," Dad yells after me.

"Wasn't funny," I call from the top of the stairs before I head to my room.

What if the baby is a people magnet—the kind of kid who hams it up for adults, sending them rolling on the floor with laughter? What if the baby is cute and funny like one of those giggling babies who gets a million hits on YouTube? What will happen to me then?

I plunk down on my bed and stare at the picture on my bureau. It shows Mom, Dad, and me in Times Square during our trip to New York last year. That was a fun vacation—the bright lights, the soft pretzels, and the best people watching ever.

I lean over to wipe the dust off the picture frame. I wish we were going somewhere fun this summer, but Mom thought it was better not to travel while she was pregnant.

Everything's already changing so much. And it's going to change even more when the baby's here.

## CHAPTER 10

As Mom pulls up to the community center, Ollie walks past our car. "Oh, who is that sweet boy?" Mom asks.

"He's in my class," I say. "But how do you know he's sweet?"

"Well, he smiled and waved goodbye to the person who dropped him off." Mom rolls down her window. "And look, he's still smiling." She points.

"Mom, stop it. He'll see you." I tap her hand down.

"It's so nice to see a boy taking up dance," Mom says as Maggie and I get out of the car.

I hit my forehead with my palm. "There are other boys in the class. Bye."

"Thanks for the ride, Mrs. Frankel," Maggie says.

"Have fun," she calls after us.

"That was a close call," I say to Maggie after we're safely inside the building. "*Are* there any boys in the dance class?"

"A couple."

"Cool."

Maggie smiles. "Do you like that kid?"

"Ugh, no. We just met."

"Are you sure?" Her smile turns into a smirk.

"Bye!" I shake my hand in front of her face.

I don't *like* Ollie, and even if I did, I'd never announce it in the middle of a hallway. Walls like these have a way of sucking up secrets and spitting them out to anyone who walks by.

By the time I step into my classroom, Mary, Sara, and Ollie are already seated. Mrs. Wrigley looks up from her computer. "Good morning, Margaret. Pick any spot you like."

I so want to correct her. I should've told her on the first day that I like to go by my middle name . . . Sydney.

There are twelve seats and seven kids in the class. If I sit next to Ollie, he might think I *like* like him. But if I sit far away from him, then he might think I *dis*like him. Tough choice.

I do the only thing that makes sense: I drop my

pencil on the floor. It rolls toward Ollie.

"I'll get that," he says, jumping up.

"Thanks." I quickly take a seat with empty chairs on either side.

Ollie hands me the pencil, slides his backpack over one seat, and sits down next to me. It worked!

He reaches into his class folder and pulls out a crisp piece of paper. "Did you do the homework?"

"Yeah. But I can't believe we have homework in the summer."

"Me neither!"

Calvin and Alice walk in and sit down at opposite ends of the room. Calvin asks for another homework paper and quickly starts filling it out. "Favorite food?" He laughs. "Too many to list."

"My thoughts exactly," Ollie says.

"Yeah," I say quietly. "And sometimes I love pizza, but then I have a kind I don't like, and then I'm not into it at all."

"I know! My mom always wants to order from Pedro's Pizza, and I don't like their crust. It's too hard. She says, 'pizza is pizza,' but that's not true."

"Same! We got pizza from there once too, and I tore the crust right off," I say.

Mrs. Wrigley claps her hands together. "I'm so

glad everyone enjoyed this assignment."

I wouldn't go that far.

"Wait! I'm almost finished," Calvin blurts out.

"Two minutes." Mrs. Wrigley holds up two fingers.

"I wrote a lot on the back," says Alice, waving her paper back and forth. It's filled with tiny, neat handwriting. My eyes hurt just looking at it.

"That's perfectly fine," Mrs. Wrigley replies. "Let's share our answers. Chime in whenever you want by raising your hand."

I wonder if we have to chime in at all. It's always tricky when teachers tell us to raise our hands when we feel like it. My third-grade teacher, Ms. Nolan, started off the year like that, but then she suddenly started calling on a couple of the quiet kids at random. If I hesitated to speak when she called on me, she'd say, "Come on, Sydney. I know you know the answer." That always made me want to shrivel up into a ball. I like warnings. There were no warnings with Ms. Nolan.

Pizza is a popular favorite food, but Alice chose tuna. And I thought *I* was going to be the strange one with an apple. I raise my hand when we get to best friends.

"My best friend is M—Sydney." Ugh, so weird. I'm my own best friend!

"And what makes Sydney such a good best friend?" Mrs. Wrigley asks.

Maggie just gets me. I love that she's friendly and doesn't have trouble talking to anyone. I guess I wish I could be like that—so free. "Um, because we never argue and always have fun together."

"Sounds like my friend Anna and me when we were growing up," Mrs. Wrigley says.

"Are you still friends?" Alice asks.

"We sure are, but now we live in different states. We talk on the phone every week and see each other at least once a year." Mrs. Wrigley points to the big map hanging on the wall. "She lives in Ohio."

My stomach drops. Once a year? That stinks. I couldn't possibly hold all my secrets for that long. Maggie had better never move away.

I wonder what it was like for Warren when he left Miami three years ago. He was friends with a couple of the boys from our school before he moved. I wouldn't mind reinventing myself like Warren has, but I wouldn't trade being near my best friend for that.

"Okay, you can put your lists away now. Thanks for sharing." Mrs. Wrigley walks over to the whiteboard. "We're going to work in partners for one more get-to-know-you exercise, and then we'll plunge into the reading activities."

I scan the room. Sara and Mary have already paired up. Alice is moving to sit by Calvin. I stare at the side of Ollie's face, hoping he'll turn to face me and ask me to be his partner. He's crouched down, fidgeting with the zipper on the small pocket of his backpack.

That's when Hailey stands up and announces, "Okay, Ollie, looks like we're going to have to work together."

Have to? That's unfair. I should've had the guts to ask Ollie before Hailey swooped in. He says yes. So basically, I'm doomed for life—the odd one out. Maybe Mrs. Wrigley will take pity on me and be my partner.

"There are seven of us in this class," Ollie says. "Since that's an odd number, let's all work together." Ollie points to Hailey and me.

I breathe a huge sigh of relief.

"Wow, you're so good at math," Hailey says to him and ignores me.

Oh, brother.

Mrs. Wrigley claps her hands again, and we all face the front. "This assignment is a fun one. Write three questions you'd like to ask your partner, and then interview them. We already learned a bit about everyone from the questionnaire, so try to dig deeper. You'll present what you learn to the group."

More presenting? That is so not part of reading. My stomach trembles. I know this is a small group, but I still don't want to talk in front of everyone. I glance over at Mary. Her lips are pursed tight. She looks even more nervous than I am. I feel bad for her.

"I've got it," Hailey says. "I'll interview Ollie, and he'll interview Margaret. Then I guess Margaret can interview me."

Ollie and I both nod. We all start working on our questions. I'm not sure what I want to know about Hailey. I already know about her big family and what she likes to eat. And by looking at her— decked out in three charm bracelets, hoop earrings, and a silver necklace—I can guess that she's super into accessories.

Hailey covers her paper as if we might steal one

of her brilliant ideas. I write down two questions but am struggling to come up with a third. I don't want to ask something stupid or something that sounds like I'm prying too much. Hailey seems easily annoyed.

"I'll start," Hailey says. Neither of us complain. "Ollie, where were you born?"

"Boston," he answers.

"Do you like cheerleaders?"

His faces scrunches up. "I don't know. Well, I don't know any personally."

Hailey beams. "You're looking at one."

"You're a cheerleader?" I butt in.

"Yeah, I've been cheering since I was four. I practically sleep with my pom-poms."

"Don't they get itchy?" I pull my glasses off and wipe them with my T-shirt—a terrible no-no according to my eye doctor. Good thing he's not here.

"I don't put them on my face or anything," Hailey says. "I have a special case for them."

"Oh, wow," is all I can think to say.

Hailey moves on and asks Ollie what he wants to be when he grows up. He says a zookeeper. That would be a cool job.

"Margaret, what's your favorite holiday?" Ollie asks me.

Hmm. That's always a tough one. I love a lot of holidays, especially the ones when we get to miss school.

"Christmas, duh," Hailey blurts.

"I don't celebrate Christmas," I say.

"How awful!" Hailey gasps. "I mean, who—"

Geez, this girl is so into herself. "I'm Jewish," I cut her off.

"I feel so bad for you," Hailey says.

"Why?" I say. "I celebrate other holidays. Like Hanukkah. I guess that's my favorite holiday."

"You're so lucky." Ollie writes down my answer. "My aunt is Jewish. We always visit her and my uncle for Hanukkah. I like lighting the menorah and eating latkes."

"Those are my favorite parts too," I say.

Next, Ollie asks me what I want to be when I grow up, and I say an entrepreneur. "I saw this show once with this guy who lived in an enormous house with a gazillion gadgets," I explain. "And this lady came over, and she asked what he did, and he said he was an entrepreneur. It means you can do whatever you want. If you change your mind, people won't say, 'Oh, I thought you did such and such,' and even if they did, you could say, 'Well, that's because I'm an entrepreneur.'"

I suddenly realize how much I've been talking. I can feel Phase 1 coming on. But it's kind of surprising that it didn't kick in earlier.

Ollie nods like everything I've said makes total sense to him. "That sounds awesome."

Hailey just stares at me.

"Last question," says Ollie. "What's the strangest food you've ever eaten?"

I look around the room to make sure no one else is listening. "It's not really people food, but once, on the way home from school, my best friend dared me to eat birdseed."

"Gross!" Hailey exclaims.

"Cool," Ollie says. "What did it taste like?"

"Kind of like sunflower seeds." I shrug. "It was no big deal."

Hailey pops a breath mint into her mouth and says, "Still gross."

Now it's my turn to question Hailey. "Where were you born?"

She sighs. "I already asked Ollie that."

Sheesh, now she thinks I stole her question.

"I wrote it down." I point to my paper.

"Well . . ." She leans in closer to us. "I was born on an airplane."

Ollie and I both gasp.

"Yeah, my mom was flying home from Paris, and the plane was right over the middle of the ocean. There was nowhere for it to land."

"That's scary," I say. I hope something like that doesn't happen to Mom. I mean, we're not planning any trips, but what if our car breaks down in the middle of the turnpike? Or what if she has the baby during a hurricane or a flood?

Okay, I'm officially freaking myself out now. I try to focus on my next question for Hailey. "What do you want to be when you grow up?"

"A princess."

"For real?" Not that I'm especially surprised.

"Yeah. I want to marry a prince, but I'll still do things like help poor kids and stuff."

"That's nice," I say. I wonder what classes she would take in college to prepare for a life of royalty. Grooming? Shopping? Hand-waving?

"I bet that would be really hard," Ollie says seriously. "If you're a princess, people expect you to look like a Barbie doll."

"And you have to wear uncomfortable high-heeled shoes," I add.

Hailey glares at me. "Well, it wouldn't be good for *you*. You're too tall. You can't be taller than the prince. It ruins the photographs."

I cross my arms. I know I'm too tall for the little-kid playground at the park or the mini roller coaster at the youth fair, but too tall to be royalty?

"That's not true," Ollie says. "My mom says it's old-fashioned to think girls can only date guys who are taller than they are."

"Royalty *is* old-fashioned!" Hailey protests.

Ollie shakes his head. "There are a lot of tall princes. Prince William is six-two. And Prince Nikolai of Denmark is a model, so he's probably tall."

I have to smile. Princess Sydney—I could get used to that.

"Whatever." Hailey rolls her eyes. "What's the last question, Margaret?"

Oh, crud. I still don't have a third one. I have no idea what to ask.

"One minute left," Mrs. Wrigley announces.

"Hello?" Hailey waves her hand in front of my face.

I look down at my feet. Then at Hailey's feet.

Mine look huge compared to hers.

"Is the question down there?" Hailey chuckles.

I know my face is red. Think fast, Sydney! "Yes." I stick out my foot in front of Hailey. "Which sock do you like better?"

"They're . . . not the same?" She gives me a funny look.

"Nope. I was in a rush this morning."

She peers down at my feet. "Um, I like the purple one, then."

Whew! My mismatched purple and green socks have saved the day!

It's time for each of us to introduce our partners to the rest of the class. I'm not as nervous as I thought I would be. Mostly because I won't be talking about myself, and I have everything written down in front of me. And since the class is small, I don't have to speak too loudly.

Our group is the last to go. Ollie tells everyone I'm cool for trying birdseed. No one laughs at me, and Calvin even gives me a thumbs-up. Hailey goes next, and then it's my turn. "Um, I interviewed Hailey. She was born on a plane flying from Paris."

A few people react with *wow*s and *omg*s. I continue, "She wants to be a princess when she grows up, and she likes my purple sock better than my green one."

"That was the best question," Ollie says.

"Thanks." I smile. This went much better than I thought it would.

At noon, I walk out of the classroom with Ollie. Hailey's in front of us, texting on her phone.

Ollie holds the door open for me. "Do you have a cell phone?"

"No." I sigh. "My parents promised to get me one at the end of the summer."

"Same here."

Ollie and I have more in common than I realized.

After I say goodbye to him, I spot a super-sweaty Maggie coming toward me. "Whoa. Did you have a solo?"

"It was tap day." She wipes her forehead with her hand. "I have to run to the bathroom and try to get rid of this sweat before your mom gets here!"

Luckily, Mom hasn't pulled up to the community center yet, so Maggie has time to pat her face and arms with paper towels.

When Mom does show up and we get into her car, she says, "Sorry I'm a little late. My doctor's appointment ran long. Did you learn anything new in class?"

"Uh-huh." I nod, braced for a follow-up question.

Maggie jumps in. "Sydney was just telling me about how her class is learning tap."

"Really?" Mom says. "Don't you need tap shoes for that?"

"Oh, I, uh, borrowed Maggie's shoes," I stammer. "Didn't I tell you that already?"

"You didn't, but that's great." Mom smiles. "I wouldn't have thought you two would have the same shoe size."

Maggie quickly changes the subject. "How big is the baby now?" Nice save!

Mom pulls out of the parking lot. "The baby's now the size of a tomato."

"You mean it shrank from a banana to a tomato?" I ask.

Mom laughs. "No—maybe I'd better pick a different example." She pauses. "More like a small eggplant."

I picture an eggplant sitting in the seat behind me. At least I won't have to take turns calling shotgun with an eggplant.

"Want to see the photo? It's in my purse."

I fish a small black-and-white picture out of her bag. It's pretty blurry, and the shape in the middle reminds me of an alien.

"Dad and I think the baby's going to look like you," Mom adds.

In other words, I look like an eggplant-sized extraterrestrial? Great.

## CHAPTER 11

Maggie and I are sitting in her room. I'm complaining about Mom, and she's trying to make me feel better by exfoliating my skin with a new avocado facial cleanser that she whipped up after watching a YouTube video on facials.

"Ever since she's been pregnant, she's been on my case about speaking up more."

Maggie massages my forehead. "Well, you did a good job speaking up on the first day of classes when she wanted to meet your teacher."

"I guess I did, but only because we were so close to having our covers blown. I was desperate."

Maggie helps me stand up. "Okay, it's been ten minutes. Go wash off the cleanser now, and your skin will be as smooth as a baby's bottom!"

"Seriously? Another thing to remind me of the baby?"

In the bathroom, I turn the water on and wash off every last speck of the baby-bottom-making cleanser from my eleven-year-old skin.

"You look good," Maggie says as I step back into her room.

"As good as Warren?" I wink.

She laughs. "Well . . ."

"You totally like him."

"I never said that."

"Please." I throw a pillow at her. "You didn't have to say it. You just breathed it."

She tosses the pillow back at me. "Well, you *walked* it." She gets up and prances around on her tippy-toes.

I crack up. "I do not walk like that." I get up too, stick out my butt, and slide across the room. "That's you."

We both walk around the room pretending to be each other until the doorbell rings. Maggie runs to her closet.

"What are you doing?"

"Hiding. Olivia's here for Shabbat dinner." Maggie slides the closet's double doors shut.

"Oh, no! You haven't seen her since you told her Jake was waiting for her outside the community center?"

"Nope."

"Ugh." I flop down onto Maggie's beanbag chair. "Maybe she forgot."

"Maybe. But I need to have a plan in case she asks me about it."

"You could tell her you *thought* Jake was outside."

"Yeah, maybe. But then she'll think I'm really stupid."

I shrug. "Nothing wrong with that."

"I guess." Maggie steps out of the closet. "But it would be better if *she* were the stupid one."

"Well, maybe she misheard what you said."

"Like, a different Jake was outside?"

"No, like . . . maybe you said there was cake outside."

"Yes!" Maggie claps her hands. "Not my fault if she ran outside for cake. Let's go."

I follow Maggie downstairs. Olivia, Jake, and Jake and Maggie's parents are sitting in the family room, stiff like zombies. I'm not sure if I ever want to go on a date, because everyone seems terrified. Even Mr. and Dr. Stein look awkward, and they've been married for like a hundred years.

Olivia says hi to us. I wonder if she's nervous

being here. I was nervous just being at Warren's house, and I don't even like him.

After a few awkward minutes, we all move to the kitchen. Dr. Stein lights the candles, and Jake says the blessing over the challah in Hebrew. When he's done, Olivia tells him he was cute.

Maggie and I roll our eyes.

We all sit down. There's enough food on the table for like twenty people.

"This is so good," I say to Maggie in between mouthfuls. Dr. Stein makes the best brisket and potatoes.

"I know. My mom went all out."

"Yeah, it feels like a Passover Seder!"

Dr. Stein peppers Olivia with a zillion questions, and I think we're in the clear until she turns to us. "Maggie, Sydney, how do you like your classes?"

"Good," Maggie says. "My teacher's really nice."

I nod. "Mine too."

"I heard that the dance class does a wonderful recital at the end of the summer," Dr. Stein says, looking at me.

Recital? Wait a minute. That can't happen. Ever.

"Are you sure?" I ask.

"Yeah," Olivia jumps in. "My friend's mom teaches that class. There's always a show at the end."

I try not to panic. The dance teacher will probably send her students home with information about the recital at some point, and Maggie won't pass it on to her parents. So as long as Mom doesn't find out somehow, we should be fine.

Olivia asks me, "Which type of dance do you like best so far?"

"Ahh . . ." Crud. Maggie and I should've traded notes before we sat down to dinner. "Zumba's fun. A good workout," I say, remembering what Bubbe told me.

"My mom does Zumba," Olivia says.

"Nice." I rip off a piece of my challah and shove it into my mouth.

"Olivia," Maggie interrupts, "I'm sorry about the other day."

"Huh?" She looks confused.

"When I told you there was cake outside."

"Cake? I thought you said *Jake*."

"I thought you might have thought that. I'd just had my braces tightened, so I probably sounded funny."

Jake finally looks up from his plate. "What are you guys talking about?"

"Nothing." Maggie waves her hand. "Can somebody pass me the challah?"

Olivia hands her the breadboard. For the rest of the meal, Maggie's parents alternate between telling stories about themselves and bombarding Olivia with questions.

After Maggie and I grab a couple of brownies for dessert, we head back to her room.

"Do you think they've kissed a lot?" I ask.

Maggie covers her eyes. "Ew, gross. I don't want to even think about it!"

"Yeah, me neither."

"And why would someone want to kiss Jake?"

"You have a point there. High schoolers are . . . inexplicable."

"Ha! Do I detect a word of the day?"

"That would be preposterous!" I laugh.

"Wait, now that's two words of the day!"

"Ludicrous! Absurd! I've got more!"

She cracks up. "Okay, I get it. How old do you think the baby's going to be before your mom makes it do word of the day?"

"She's started already! When she reads the words out loud, she'll say, *You hear that, little one?* She even spells them for the baby."

Maggie laughs. "Maybe the baby has a mini keyboard and takes notes."

I flop down onto my stomach. "Do you think the baby's listening to us, like, all the time?"

"You mean how God listens to us?" Maggie joins me on the floor.

"No, through my mom's stomach. I think babies have very good hearing."

"I'm sure the baby hears stuff, but I think it mostly just sleeps."

I stretch out all the way on the carpet. "I could get used to that."

"We couldn't hang out, then. No Frankelstein."

I spring up. "Unless we were twins."

"That would be awesome."

"A girl in my class is having twins."

Maggie's eyes bug out. "She is?"

"No, not *her*. She's our age. Her mom is."

"That's cool. I'd like to have a twin."

"It'd be fun, especially if we were identical and could switch places on people. You could give all the oral presentations, and I could do all the underground spy stuff."

"I think that only happens in movies."

I look up at the glow-in-the-dark stars on Maggie's

ceiling. They're patiently waiting for it to get dark so they can shine. "You're probably right. Well, we're *almost* like sisters." I hold up my pinkie.

Maggie hooks her pinkie with mine. "Separated at birth!"

## CHAPTER 12

Today's Friday, and the Pendlers are coming over for lunch after my class. Mom wants me to get to know Warren better. I told her Maggie would die if she knew I was having Warren over without her, so Mom said she could come by after we eat.

I'm still annoyed at Mom for telling Warren about my summer class. But it's hard to stay mad when the scent of chocolate chip cookies is wafting up your nose.

"Mom," I say as I walk into the kitchen, "we should have guests more often. I love your cookies."

"I'm glad. This is going to be fun."

I grit my teeth. "Maybe for you. But what am I going to talk to Warren about?" When you invite someone to your house, you're supposed to be the conversation starter. It's the polite thing to do. I read that in one of Mom's magazines.

"School, sports, books."

"Okay, that would be weird. I can't just start talking about stuff like that out of nowhere."

"Hmm." She looks at my T-shirt. "Llamas and hearts. You could talk about that."

"Come on, Mom, be serious."

"I'm sure you'll find things to chat about. Just relax."

Easy for her to say.

"Humph." I open the cutlery drawer and take out some knives and forks. "Just please don't say anything about my dance class this time." I lean down and talk to her belly. "You neither."

"All right, all right."

The doorbell rings, and Mom asks me to get it. As soon as I open the door, Warren hands me a plate of brownies.

"Thanks! Did you make these?"

"No, but I'll eat them." He laughs.

"Me too," I say and lead him and his mom into the kitchen. Mom and Mrs. Pendler hug as if they haven't seen each other in years.

"My mom has been very huggy ever since she got pregnant," I say to Warren.

"Oh, my mom's always like that! If I don't hug

her goodbye every morning before school, I'm in trouble."

Good thing we can walk to Coral Rock Middle, or he would have to hug her in front of the school building, where a bunch of other kids could see.

I definitely don't want Mom walking me to middle school—especially because she'd probably try to talk to all my teachers—but I also don't love the idea of going by myself. In all the middle schools on TV shows, kids are running down the hallways at full speed. Like if you stop for even a minute to find your way, you'll be plowed over. Okay, so I might be one of the tallest sixth-graders, but that just means I have farther to fall, which makes it that much more embarrassing.

Warren and I hang at the kitchen counter— I lean forward, and he leans back. I wait for him to talk, but instead, I see him eyeing the food that's set up on the table.

I try to think of something to talk about. Anything. But my brain feels like a blank slate. No words come to mind.

My face feels hot. I know I'm red and my breathing is getting shallow. I have to say something.

Anything. School. That's it! You can always talk about school.

I blurt, "It's going to be a lot different at Coral Rock Middle. I see kids hanging around outside all the time."

"Yeah, and my cousin told me that the lunches are actually rejects from Eastman Academy."

"Seriously? Like the lunches kids didn't eat? Nasty!" I picture lunch trays stacked high with moldy burgers and stale french fries. So far, middle school stinks.

"I know. I'm going to bring mine from home."

"Smart. Me too."

Mom calls us to lunch. I exhale. That wasn't as bad as I thought it was going to be. Warren and I actually did find something to talk about.

Lunch consists of a lot of chewing and passing food. Plus, Mom and Mrs. Pendler can go on forever about the baby. I'm kind of off the hook there. When Mom puts out her chocolate chip cookies and Mrs. Pendler's brownies and refills our lemonade glasses, she asks Warren if he's nervous about going to middle school.

"Nah. I want to try out for the basketball team, and I can't wait to have a locker."

"That's great," Mom says.

"What about you, Sydney?" Mrs. Pendler asks.

"Uh . . ." I pause.

"Nervous, I'd say," Mom answers for me. "Sydney can be very shy."

I cover my face with my hands. What part of *don't embarrass me* does Mom not get?

I don't need someone to hand me a mirror to tell me my face is red. A Phase 2 for sure.

Mrs. Pendler smiles at me. "I don't blame you. It's always daunting going to a new school. But middle school does offer more freedom."

At least Mrs. Pendler gets me, but I need to change the subject before Mom says anything else.

I look around the room for ideas. My eye catches the ceramic rooster on top of the counter. "Do you like roosters?"

Everyone looks at me like I'm an alien.

"Yes." Mrs. Pendler nods.

"Cool. I was thinking of painting a picture of one to go in our kitchen."

"That's a lovely idea," Mom says. "We could use some fresh artwork around here."

"Would you make one for me too?" asks Mrs. Pendler. "It would go great with all my red appliances."

Oh, no. What have I gotten myself into? I glance over at Warren. He must think I'm beyond weird now.

"I wish I could paint," he says.

Me too. Where is Ollie with his calming hand lotion when I need it?

## CHAPTER 13

The doorbell rings while we're finishing dessert. Maggie's here! I run to get the door.

Maggie's wearing a white top and a green skirt. She never wears a skirt. Ever.

"I know what you're thinking," she whispers. "But my mom bought this outfit for me last Passover, and I figured I should wear it. You know, before it goes out of style."

"Sure." I smile. "He's in the kitchen."

I sneak a quick peek in the hallway mirror. My face is not as bad as I thought. The pink could definitely pass as a minor sunburn.

We all sit in the family room. Warren plunks down on the couch, Maggie and I share the loveseat. I'm surprised Maggie doesn't sit next to him, but I figure she has the jitters.

"How was living in Chicago?" she asks Warren.

"It was cool."

"The weather or the place?" Maggie jokes awkwardly.

"Well, both. It was really cold in the winter, but I liked my school." He picks up a stack of coasters that we got on our visit to New York last year and shuffles through them. I make a mental note not to leave anything embarrassing lying around, because Warren is sure to play with it.

Maggie tilts her head to the left. "You dress differently than you used to."

Warren looks down at his black T-shirt and red gym shorts. "Oh."

I'm embarrassed for him.

He touches his head. He totally knows we're thinking about the sweatbands. But it's not just his clothes that are different. He's different too.

Maggie leans forward. "Do you want to go to the movies with us this weekend?"

"Uh, sure. I think I'm free Sunday. How about the race car movie?"

"Yes," Maggie and I agree. Even though we made a list of the movies we wanted to see the other day and the race car movie tied for last place with the movie about the guy who falls asleep at the noodle factory.

We talk about movies and school and the best kind of sandwich. I do a lot of listening, but I do some talking too, especially when it gets to sandwiches. Warren is a fellow tuna hoagie lover. By the time Warren leaves, I'm about to explode with excitement. I can't believe we're going to the movies with him.

Maggie and I hang around in the family room doodling. I'm thinking about the roosters I'm supposed to draw. I hope Mom and Mrs. Pendler have short memories.

Mom sits down on the couch with a cooking magazine. "I'm exhausted. But that was nice."

I don't respond. I still can't believe she told the Pendlers I was shy and nervous.

"Yeah!" Maggie says. "We asked Warren to go with us to the movies on Sunday."

"You mean *you* did," I say. "Will you take us, Mom?"

She raises her eyebrows. "You want me to go with you?"

That would be a fate worse than death.

"You could see a different movie," Maggie suggests.

Mom takes a sip of her lemonade. "I'll talk to your

mom and Mrs. Pendler about the arrangements."

"Cool," we both say.

I'm excited for Maggie. This is the closest that either of us has gotten to hanging out with a boy.

## CHAPTER 14

While we're eating breakfast on Saturday morning, Mom tells me how glad she is that Maggie and I are branching out. I don't do much talking because I'm still annoyed with her for embarrassing me in front of the Pendlers yesterday.

"Why so quiet?" Dad finally asks me.

"No reason. Just tired."

"Must be all that dancing you're doing in class," Mom says.

"Ah, yeah." I shove a huge spoonful of cereal into my mouth.

"Which is your favorite style of dance so far?" Dad asks.

I know I can't say Zumba because then they'll probably make me have a FaceTime Zumba party with Bubbe.

"Hip-hop," I blurt.

Technically, it's not lying. I went to a hip-hop-themed birthday party once, and it was a lot of fun. After that, I practiced the routine in my room every night for a few weeks.

Mom picks up the cereal box and starts clearing the table. "But she still hasn't worn any of the new outfits I bought her."

"Everyone dresses casual," I say.

"Let her be," Dad says.

"Okay, fine." Mom sighs.

I'm going to have to make sure she doesn't see my homework from reading class. We have a short story to read, plus another assignment on top of that. We're supposed to do something outside our comfort zone this weekend and then tell the class about it on Monday.

"Are you excited for tomorrow?" Dad asks.

"We're just going to the movies with Warren. Nothing special."

"Well, you two seemed pretty excited yesterday." Mom laughs.

"That was all Maggie. You know how she is." I look at the word of the day. "She's very *exuberant*."

"Exuberant because . . . ? Complete the sentence, please."

Argh, Mom needs to go back to teaching. "Maggie's exuberant because she can't wait to go to the movies with her friends."

"A-plus." Mom kisses me on the forehead. "Oh, you feel warm."

"Really? I'm fine. I was actually going to put on a sweatshirt. It's kind of cold in here with the AC running."

"And carrying this baby has made me hot all the time." Mom fans herself.

"Did you always feel hot when I was in your stomach?" I ask.

"Well, it wasn't as bad because I wasn't pregnant with you in the middle of the summer."

I carry my empty cereal bowl to the sink and realize I feel a little dizzy. "I'm going up to my room to relax."

I don't know what that baby's doing to Mom, but this house is freezing. I pull out a long-sleeve T-shirt from my drawer and throw it on. A minute later, I dig out three more shirts. I double up on socks too, but I still feel like I'm full of icicles.

It's time to break out the winter gear I wear a total of three days a year here in Miami. I slide on my red winter hat and striped gloves. But my face is still cold. I dive under my sheets and comforter. Is Mom trying to freeze me out of this house? We're not only aliens—we also hail from an arctic planet.

A few minutes later, Mom walks into my room. "What's going on?"

I stick my head out of my blanket cave. "I'm freezing. Can you bring me some polar bear fur?"

Mom slowly pulls back my comforter. "What on earth are you doing?"

"Trying to get warm."

"You do know it's almost ninety degrees outside?"

"For real? I'm wearing seven shirts, two pairs of socks, pajama pants, a winter hat, and mittens." I suddenly feel exhausted. Even talking seems like a lot of effort.

Mom frowns and puts her hand on my forehand. "You're hot. You have a fever."

Oh, no. "Does that mean—?"

"Yes, I'm afraid so. No movies tomorrow."

"But that's in like eighteen hours!" I whine.

"I'm sorry, but it's not enough time."

"People can fly across the world in that amount of time."

Mom shakes her head.

"It's true. I saw it on the Travel Channel," I say with my eyes closed, because my lids feel like steel doors.

"I'm not debating that, Sydney. But you're sick, and you have to be fever-free for twenty-four hours before you even leave the house."

"Urgh." I bury my head in my pillow.

Mom leaves the room while I snuggle under my comforter and try to get warm. A second later, she's back with a thermometer and a bottle of Tylenol. I stick the thermometer under my tongue and pray it comes out at 98.6.

It beeps, and Mom pulls it out of my mouth. "Yep: 101.5."

"Maybe the thermometer is busted."

"Get some rest, honey. You can go to the movies another day." She pours the medicine into the plastic cup and hands it to me.

I let the purple liquid slip slowly down my throat. I consider arguing, but my tongue sinks like a paperweight and my eyes sting. I figure I'll get a little rest and see how I feel in a bit.

When I wake up, I think it's going to be dark out, but it's actually light. I look at my clock and realize I slept all day and through the night. I glance down at the floor. Five of my seven shirts are in a heap on my carpet along with my hat, gloves, and socks. I don't remember taking them off.

After I wrap myself in my comforter, I head downstairs. I would say I'm feeling better except that my head is still clogged and my body feels like it's running out of batteries. I grab a Gatorade and crash on the family room couch.

"Whoa, Dad, what are you doing here?" I ask.

He looks up from reading news on the iPad. "Wanted to get an early start. I'm off to the gym soon, and then I'm pressure washing the patio today. How's the patient?"

"Okay, but I'm bummed I can't go to the movies." I had a chance to have some real fun, and my body blew it.

"There will be plenty of movies and plenty of boys." Dad smiles.

"Ew, Dad. It's not like I'm into Warren at all. I just wanted to go to the movies."

Dad sets the iPad down. "Really? What movie?"

"Uh, the race car one. Okay, I don't actually want to see the movie."

"Hmm." He smiles. "Well, tell you what. Next time, maybe you could suggest a movie you think *you'll* like. It's good to be flexible with your friends, but it's also good to speak your mind."

I roll my eyes. "Whatever, Dad. I was just going for the popcorn, okay?"

"Makes sense to me, *sheyne meydl.*"

## CHAPTER 15

I call when I know Maggie's up. She never sleeps past eight.

"Do you want the bad news or the good news first?" I ask.

"Give me the bad. I'm ready to take whatever you have to dish out."

"I can't go to the movies this afternoon. I had a fever yesterday, and I'm still sick."

"Seriously?" she screams into the phone. I pull it a good distance away from my ear.

"Yeah, why would I make that up? My head hurts, and my bones are all achy."

"Ugh, I hope you feel better soon. It won't be the same without you."

"Aw, thanks." I sniffle.

"What's the good news?"

"You're going to be alone with Warren!"

"Oh, don't scare me." She laughs. "But I think Warren's brother, Mark, is coming too."

"Promise to call right when you get home," I say.

"Of course!"

We hang up, and my mind wanders to my reading class homework. It's already Sunday, so I need to do it soon. I wonder if getting sick counts as doing something outside my comfort zone.

Just after lunchtime, Mom agrees to go get me a cherry Slurpee, and I'm left alone for a glorious twenty minutes. What should I do with this taste of freedom?

I start by turning on the TV, since Mom's always trying to limit my screen time. Next, I get up from the couch and make myself a bowl of ice cream. And of course, I need a drink to wash it down.

Ten minutes are left, and I'm sipping orange juice, gazing at the TV, and sucking down my bowl of chocolate chip ice cream. But now what?

I know—I should call someone. But who? I would call Maggie, but she's already at the movies with Warren. My other friends from school, Lily and Gaby, are both at sleepaway camp. Calling either of my grandparents is not exciting, no offense.

I guess I'll do my reading class homework. I pull

out my folder and spot the class list inside. Ollie's number is in there. I should totally call him! It would be a great challenge for my assignment. Calling a boy is definitely out of my comfort zone.

I stare at the phone and then at Ollie's number. Seven minutes left. I can do this. I run the conversation over in my head. I just need to ask for him, then tell him who I am. Then ask him a question about the homework. After that, I can thank him and tell him I have to go. And the best thing about the phone is that it doesn't matter if my face turns red, because nobody can see me.

Five minutes of freedom left, and I dial his number. I take a deep breath as it rings. And rings again. Oh, no—I didn't think about the caller ID. It's going to come up as my dad, Aaron Frankel. How am I going to explain why it doesn't say Stein?

"Hi." A girl answers the phone. A girl. I was not prepared for that! He said he didn't have any siblings.

"Hello?" The girl sounds annoyed.

"Is Ollie there?" I ask.

"Yeah. Hold on. AWW-LEE, phone."

I can hear him breathing. My body goes stiff. "Hello."

"Hi, Ollie? It's S—Margaret."

No answer. Is he staring at the phone and wondering who Aaron Frankel is?

"From reading class."

"Oh, hi. How are you?"

"Good."

"Can you hold on a sec?"

I look at the clock. Two minutes. "Okay."

I hear muffled whispering. I bet he's talking to the girl who answered the phone. Hope he's not talking about me.

"Sorry about that. My sitter and I are about to watch a movie."

Aha, she's his sitter. I was thinking more like evil twin.

"No problem. I just wanted to ask if you knew how long the homework had to be."

"I'm not sure . . ." I hear paper shuffling. "Guess it depends on what you do. Probably a couple paragraphs or something." More paper shuffling. "Wait, it says a page long."

"Great." I'm starring right at it. It sure does.

One minute. I hear Mom's car pull into the garage.

"Thanks, Ollie. I'll see you tomorrow."

"Yeah, see you tomorrow," he says cheerfully.

I hang up and rush my bowl over to the sink before Mom walks in with my Slurpee.

"Thanks, Mom," I say when she hands it to me. I take a huge gulp of the cherry-flavored drink.

"You're looking better," she says.

"Feeling a little better too." Now that I've talked to Ollie.

I can't believe I actually called him, which is totally awesome, except . . . Oh, crud, this is not good. If I talked to him for my assignment, then I'm going to have to tell the whole class about how calling him was my big accomplishment. Then everyone will think I have a crush on Ollie, which is totally not true.

Geez, how stupid could I be?

# CHAPTER 16

I need to talk to Maggie. She's the only person I can tell about my phone call with Ollie. I doubt Mom would understand how terrible my situation is. I think grown-ups go through a machine that erases everything that was a big deal to them when they were kids and replaces it with the phrase, "There's nothing wrong with that."

In third grade, my zipper was unzipped like half the day. When I told Mom, she said it happens to everyone. For the next week, I checked, and I didn't see one kid with their zipper down. She said the same thing in fourth grade when I forgot to wear bike shorts under my skirt and did a flip at recess. She said it was no big deal, but having fifteen kids laugh in your face about the pattern on your undies is a big deal. I didn't wear a skirt for the rest of the school year.

Dad comes home from the gym and sits down next to me. He smells like a whole PE class. "How's my sweetheart doing?"

"Okay."

"I know you wanted to go to the movies with your friends, but I can take you when you're feeling better."

"Thanks, Dad." I lean on his shoulder, trying not to breathe in his workout odor. "But one thing . . ."

"What is it?"

"Can you shower?" I plug my nose.

He laughs. "What, you don't like my new cologne? It's called Real Man."

"Demand your money back."

"That's how I know you're my daughter—you have my sense of humor." He pinches my cheek and heads upstairs.

I conk out on the couch and don't wake up until I hear Mom calling me to pick up the phone in the kitchen. It's four o'clock. That means Maggie is back from the movies.

"Did you kiss, Frankelstein?" I immediately ask.

"Huh? What?" a guy's voice says.

I shrink down to a tiny particle. "Wait . . . is this Warren?"

"Yeah."

118

"Oh, sorry. I, ah, didn't expect you to call."

"My mom asked me to—well, I wanted to know how you're feeling."

Like a complete idiot. "I'm okay. Getting some rest."

"Awesome."

"Thanks for calling."

"Yeah, see you later." He hangs up.

What else can go wrong? I should just quit using the telephone forever.

A second later, the phone rings again. I don't even want to look at the thing, but I can hear Mom asking me to answer it.

I peel my hands off my eyes and glance at the caller ID. Oh, it's Maggie. I quickly answer. "Hi."

"Hi, Syd. Are you okay? You sound sick."

"Well, I am, and now I'm sicker than ever." I prop up a couch pillow behind my head.

"Oh, no. Don't tell me you're dying, because I couldn't take that."

"I'm not dying. Unless a person can die from extreme embarrassment—then I'm six feet under."

Maggie gasps. "What are you talking about? I thought you stayed home all day."

"I did. But let's just say the phone is my enemy."

I tell her about my assignment and my call with Ollie and then about how I called Warren Frankelstein. I leave out the kissing part—no need for Maggie to join my red-faced club.

"Okay," she says, "let's start with Warren. You have to admit that's pretty funny." I can tell she's holding in a laugh.

"Yeah, but I still felt like hiding my head in a paper bag."

"He probably thinks he didn't hear you right. And besides, boys forget things easily. Like if my mom tells Jake to take out the garbage and then someone texts him, Jake never remembers the garbage."

"True." But still I wish I could undo the phone call.

"Okay, and your assignment—that's no biggie. I think it's awesome that you called Ollie. He sounds cute." I hear barking on the other line. "See, even Butter agrees."

"I can't believe you're bringing your dog into this." I laugh. "But seriously, how am I going to tell the whole class about calling him?"

"Say you have a fear of the phone and you called him for the assignment. If you make it seem like he's just another person, then no one will be suspicious."

I sit up. "Good point. You always make everything seem so simple."

"No problem. That's my job as the Stein half of Frankelstein," Maggie says.

Things would be so much easier if I didn't hate speaking in public. Some people might think I'm not social, but really that's not it. I'd love to be able to speak in front of a whole group without worrying, but the truth is, I do worry. I worry that my voice will sound weird or that I'll say the wrong thing or that nothing will come out of my mouth.

"Okay, I can't believe we've been talking about me this whole time. How was the movie?"

"The movie wasn't as bad as I thought it would be."

"Who cares about the *movie* part? What about Warren? Were you alone?" I shriek.

"Not even close. Mark went too, and he invited Jake. They're only a year apart, so I guess they're friends now."

For the first time all day, I'm kind of happy I'm sick.

## CHAPTER 17

Okay, being home sick gets old fast. I'd never admit this to Mom, but I'm actually glad to be getting out of the house on Monday, even if it's to go to my summer class.

A fresh word of the day is staring me in the face when I walk into the kitchen. *Fortitude.* Yeah, the words on the board are definitely not there by accident. Mom doesn't put any old thing down. No, these words are hand selected for me. *Fortitude* means strength of mind. Courage.

I'm still nervous about sharing in class today, but I remember what Maggie said—to just play it cool.

Mom makes the best pancakes, and a whole stack is waiting for me. I eat three and am totally stuffed. I stay at the table in a food coma while Mom finishes eating.

"Have you made any friends in the dance class yet?" Mom asks.

My guilt-o-meter spikes. I wish I could tell her I'm in the reading class. But there's no way she would understand. I think of silent Mary; Calvin, who shouts things out; Hailey, who can't stop talking about herself; Sara, the girl with the robot voice; and Alice, who's trying hard to be somebody important. I think of Ollie, whose backpack is filled with toiletries.

I shrug. "Ollie's nice." It was cool to hear his voice on the phone, even if I probably sounded like a weirdo.

"Ollie?"

"Yes, the boy you saw in front of the community center. He has a pet turtle." I get up and stick my plate in the sink. "Mom, can I have a turtle?"

It would be fun to have a few small animals. I could line up their tanks in the family room, and they could all watch TV with me, or I could read to them.

"I don't think so. I can only handle one newcomer at a time."

The baby's not even born yet, and it's already ruining things for me. I should start plotting my revenge. Maybe I won't give it any of my hand-me-down toys. Not even stubby crayons.

Mr. Stein drives Maggie and me to the community center. We run into Ollie as we're walking inside. "Hi!" says Maggie. "Are you Ollie? I'm Sydney."

She doesn't stumble over my name at all. If I didn't know better, I'd never guess that she was lying.

"Hi," he says to her, but he's already looking at me. "Are you okay, Margaret?"

"Um, yeah, I'm fine. Just a little mad at the baby."

His eyes go wide. "Your mom had the baby?"

"No, but it's already pushing its way into my life. I asked my mom if I could get a turtle, and she said that would be hard with the baby coming."

"That stinks," says Ollie.

We get to our classroom door, and I wave good-bye to Maggie.

Inside, Sara is pacing up and down the rows of desks. "Hi, Sara," Ollie says.

"Hell-o, Ol-lie," she says with her eyes glued to the floor.

"Everything okay?" he asks.

"Lit-tle sad," she says.

She's wearing the same red shirt and navy shorts that she always wears. They look like a school uniform with no logo. She usually has a red bow in her hair, but not today.

"What's wrong?" Ollie asks.

"My cat, Lou-ey, is sick."

"I'm sorry," both Ollie and I say.

She stops pacing and slinks into her seat.

Ollie unzips his book bag and pulls out a small baggie with a couple of flat, green lollipops in it. He walks over to Sara. "For you."

"Thank you." Sara's pulling off the wrapper when Mrs. Wrigley enters the class. I wait for her to tell Sara to throw the pop away, but she doesn't. Instead, she goes to the file cabinet at the back of the room.

I whisper to Ollie, "That was really nice of you."

He shrugs. "It's no big deal. Those pops used to always cheer me up. My dad would bring me a bunch from the bank every Friday when I was little. Now I just carry them for emergencies."

"You carry a lot of things for emergencies," I say.

"I like to be prepared."

Calvin walks by us and waves on the way to his seat. We both wave back. I wonder what he did for his homework challenge.

Mrs. Wrigley asks who would like to share first, and Calvin shouts, "Me!" Mrs. Wrigley tells him he needs to raise his hand. He does, and she says okay.

"On Saturday, I asked two kids on my street to play with me."

"That's great. And what happened?" Mrs. Wrigley asks.

"They said yes!" Calvin jumps up from his desk. His excitement is contagious. I feel like jumping out of my seat too.

"That's wonderful. What did you play?" Mrs. Wrigley asks.

"I invited them to see my tree fort. It has a lookout tower and a windup clock in it. Then we played kickball." He swings his leg like he's kicking a ball.

"You have a tree fort?" Ollie asks. "That's so cool."

"Yeah, my dad built it. It has fourteen steps," Calvin says.

"How did you feel after you asked the kids to play?" Mrs. Wrigley asks.

"Happy!" Calvin pumps his fists in the air.

"I'm glad it worked out." Mrs. Wrigley gives him a thumbs-up.

"Yeah, but then I wanted them to leave because

it was TV time. I don't miss any wrestling matches."
He settles back into his seat and puts the air into an
imaginary headlock.

We all laugh.

"Use the DVR," Hailey says. "The thing saved
my social life." She has an answer for everything.
And she has a social life!

Mrs. Wrigley asks for the next volunteer to share.

It's no surprise that it's Hailey. "I helped Ms.
Crow from across the street carry her groceries
inside."

"That's very nice of you, but how did you find
this a challenge?" Mrs. Wrigley leans back against
her desk, arms folded.

"Well, you said to do something nice."

"Actually, the assignment was to do something
that was outside of your comfort zone."

Hailey looks down at her nails. The pink polish on one finger is chipped. "It was outside of my
comfort zone because I had to sacrifice my time to
help her."

What else did she have to do? Meet with her personal shopper?

I notice that Mary's pale. I hope she's okay. I consider raising my hand and telling Mrs. Wrigley, but

I definitely don't want to embarrass Mary, because I know how that feels.

Alice's hand shoots up. "I passed the deepwater swimming test at the lake near my grandparents' house. You have to take the test if you want to swim out to the floating dock. I failed it two summers ago and was afraid to try again."

"That's terrific determination," Mrs. Wrigley says. "Now who's next?"

When no hands shoot up, she calls on Ollie. I'm spared, but I know it's only for a couple of minutes.

"Well . . ." Ollie says, staring at the floor. His right hand is tucked under his leg. I've never seen him so nervous before. I feel bad. As if I should do something. Maybe my nerves are contagious. I peek at his face, but it's not red.

"Are you okay?" I whisper.

He doesn't answer me but instead says, "Mine didn't go so well."

Mrs. Wrigley walks closer to his desk. "That's okay, Ollie. Things don't always go as planned. It's how we deal with them that matters."

"Yeah!" Calvin shouts.

Mrs. Wrigley turns to Calvin and motions for him to keep quiet.

"Would you like us to skip you today?" She places her hand on Ollie's desk.

"No, it's okay. No one's going to laugh, right?"

Everyone says no. Mary even gives him a thumbs-up. I wish I could reach into my bag and give him something special, like how he gave Sara the lollipop. But all I have is a pencil and my dance-themed class folder.

"I tried to use my cousin's electric scooter and fell flat on my face."

Calvin stands up and looks at Ollie. "Your face isn't messed up."

"I wore a helmet, but I did scrape my chin." He points to the faint red mark.

Hailey stands up too. "Yeah, I can't see anything. Are you wearing makeup?"

Calvin laughs at that. Mrs. Wrigley gives him a stern look.

"Just a little something from my bag." Ollie pats the side of his trusty backpack.

"I fell off a horse once and got all scraped up," Alice says.

"You rode a horse?" Ollie asks. "Lucky!"

"That's nothing." Hailey flashes us a huge smile. "I've ridden horses, llamas, elephants, an ape . . ."

Okay, that's impossible. She's so annoying.

"How do you ride an ape?" Ollie asks. I picture Hailey on the ape's back waving her pom-poms back and forth. Then I picture the ape zooming up the tree and leaving Hailey stuck in a high branch. I laugh to myself.

"Hailey, it's Ollie's turn to share. Please continue," Mrs. Wrigley says.

Ollie sighs. "I have bad hand-eye coordination. It's called dyspraxia. It makes me seem like a klutz because I fall or bump into things a lot. Wearing glasses helps, but it gets worse when I'm stressed, and I stress myself out a lot."

He lowers his head onto his desk. His thin blond hair falls straight, like dry angel hair spaghetti.

"I know how you feel," I whisper. I'm not sure if he hears me, but I hope he does.

Mrs. Wrigley says, "It's okay. We don't score every time. You just have to get out there and give it another try."

"That's exactly what my mom said." Ollie sighs.

Now I feel even stupider. Most people are talking about real things, things that are serious, and I'm talking about phone anxiety. It's not a medical condition. It's just embarrassing.

"Margaret, are you ready to share?" Mrs. Wrigley asks.

I nod but immediately feel heat rising to my face. I need to get my own calming lotion.

I might as well get it over with. I take a deep breath. "I made a phone call."

"And?" Hailey says. "I do that all the time." She flashes her cell phone to the group.

Sheesh, why can't she mind her own business?

"Let her finish," Mrs. Wrigley warns.

I focus my eyes on the door. My escape. "I'm not a phone person. I don't have my own phone. But I got up the fortitude to make a call . . ."

"You had to fart and toot?!" Calvin bursts out laughing.

Geez, he's so immature. "I said I had the *fort-i-tude* to call Ollie about the homework."

"You like Ol-lie?" Sara asks.

"Duh!" Calvin shouts.

"Obvious," Alice sings.

My face is on fire. I try to breathe deep again. It's not working. "No way! That's stupid," I snap.

Ollie slumps in his chair. Oh, no. I think I hurt his feelings.

"I meant it took fortitude to call him because I

don't like calling people."

"Thanks for sharing," Mrs. Wrigley says. "Talking on the phone can be very intimidating for a lot of people. I'm glad you called someone you felt comfortable with."

Then why do I feel so bad now? My face is like a fireball.

"Margaret, are you okay? Your face is very red, and your breathing sounds shaky," Mrs. Wrigley says.

Oh, great. My face is definitely at least a Phase 4. I take a couple of short breaths. "I'm okay."

She takes a piece of paper from her desk and scribbles on it. "I'm sending you to the nurse just to make sure."

I nod and take the slip of paper. I know the nurse can't do anything, but at least I can get out of this room until my face and breathing go back to normal.

"Sara, why don't you go with Margaret?" Mrs. Wrigley says. "She could use a buddy."

Sara nods and follows me out the door. We walk down the hallway to the back of the building. The halls are empty since everyone is in class. As we walk, my breathing slows to normal.

"You will be o-kay," Sara says as I push through the double doors to the nurse's office.

"Yes. Thanks." I would've been fine hiding out in the bathroom for ten minutes, but since Sara's my chaperone, I'm stuck here.

The nurse is sitting at a small desk up front. She's really old, like older than my bubbe.

"Hello. How can I help you?" she asks.

I hand her the piece of paper from Mrs. Wrigley.

She stands up. I didn't expect her to be so short. I don't even think she reaches my shoulders. I feel like a giant.

"You are o-kay," Sara repeats.

"Yes. You can go back to class," I say.

She nods and takes off.

I peer at the nurse's name tag: *Ms. Gamble.* That's a pretty risky name for a nurse.

After reading the note, she shuffles over to the filing cabinet a few feet from her desk. "Have a seat on the bench," she says with her back to me.

Is it too late to make a break for it? I'm confident I could outrun her.

I decide against the great escape and hoist myself onto the examination table. I wonder what they're talking about in class now. Hopefully not about me and my red face. And I hope Ollie doesn't hate me.

Ms. Gamble grabs a manila file folder and walks over to me. "Do you feel faint?" she asks.

"Nope."

"Has this happened before?"

"Uh, yes, but it goes away pretty quickly." I try to reassure her, so I can get out of here fast.

"Hmm." She opens the folder and starts reading. "Margaret Stein."

I don't say anything. If I don't answer, then technically I'm not lying.

"Oh, it says you're allergic to salmon. Have you eaten salmon today?"

"Nope."

"Did you come into contact with salmon?"

"Nope."

She glances over at me and back at the file. Back at me.

I feel my face getting hot again. What is she looking for? "I'm fine." I gulp.

"Your form says you're five-one and you weigh . . ." She trails off. "I must have the wrong folder." She closes it and looks at the name on the outside again.

Ugh. I bunch up my shoulders, hoping that makes me look slightly shorter. "No, that's me. I eat a lot of pasta. It helps me grow."

"Twenty pounds and six inches," she says. "That would be a big change in the couple of weeks since your parents filled out these forms."

Oh, man, I have to think fast! "My mom is five-one, so she probably was thinking about herself when she filled out the form."

"Parents really need to take this paperwork more seriously." She shakes her head and flips through the rest of the file. "Well, your mom's a doctor. I'll give her a call to see what she thinks."

"Why? I'm feeling fine. I was just hot."

"She might want to check in with you."

"No, she's in surgery right now."

"Surgery?" She looks at my file again. "But it says here that she's a family doctor."

Ms. Gamble is staring at me as if she's waiting for me to crack.

"Patient confidentiality. I don't even know. Can I go back to class?"

She looks me up and down. "I don't know, Margaret. This looks like some pretty serious skin irritation. It could be a reaction to something . . ."

Aha! I've got it. "Can you keep a secret?"

She narrows her eyes. I'll take that as a yes.

"My mom bought some new cream from a local farm, and I tried it on my face. It turned out to be foot cream! I'm so embarrassed, so please don't tell anyone."

She cracks a thin smile. "You have to read labels."

"I know. I'll be more careful."

"Here you go." She hands me back the hall pass with her signature, and I run out of there before she changes her mind.

That was a close call. I take deep breaths all the way down the hallway. I've been watching Mom practice her breathing in preparation for delivering the baby. It's supposed to make you feel relaxed. And I don't want Mrs. Wrigley to send me back to Ms. Gamble. I've had enough drama for one day.

When I get to class, only two minutes are left on the clock. I look over at Ollie. He's organizing the pencils in his bag. I wonder if he's mad at me for saying I didn't like him. But that's totally not what I meant.

"Ollie, I'm glad I called you," I say.

"Why, because I'm organized?"

"Yeah—I mean, no. I mean, it's awesome that you're organized, but I called you because I like you as a friend."

"Okay." He looks up at me with his big brown teddy bear eyes. "And let me guess: Now that you know I have this dumb problem, you don't like me anymore."

"No, that's not true at all!"

Ollie looks angry. He probably thinks I'm a jerk. I should explain that new situations make me anxious.

But there's no time. Mrs. Wrigley informs us that class is over.

I peer at Ollie. All we need to do is make eye contact. Share a smile. Anything. I just don't want him to be mad at me. But he's staring straight at Mrs. Wrigley. I can't believe I upset him so much.

"Before you all leave," Mrs. Wrigley says, "I'm going to pass out the book we'll be reading together and at home." She pulls a stack of books out from behind her desk. I recognize the cover image. It's *Wonder* by R. J. Palacio. I love that book.

Mrs. Wrigley holds up a copy. "How many of you have read this?" Only Mary and I raise our hands.

"Did you like it?"

We both nod. I smile at Mary, and she smiles back.

"Now, how many people have seen the movie?" she asks.

Alice and Hailey raise their hands along with Mary and me.

"Well, that's great. You'll be coming to this book with prior knowledge, which will make the reading easier. As you read, I want you to focus on the feelings of the characters. The reason I had you do all the self-awareness exercises is that in order to understand and sympathize with those around us, we have to get to know ourselves first."

I thought this was a reading improvement class, not a *self*-improvement class. But at least I'll be rereading a book I love. And it's a good thing I have a copy of the book at home, because Maggie's supposed to be reading too.

Mrs. Wrigley hands out the books and asks us to read the first three chapters for homework. It's time to leave.

Ollie's taking forever to get his backpack reorganized, so I wait for him right outside the door. I'm just going to say sorry again. I don't know what else to do.

While he's busy with his backpack, Mrs. Wrigley calls him over to her desk.

"Ready to go?" Maggie practically slams into me.

"Uh . . ." I stare into my classroom.

"You do like him, don't you?" Maggie says.

"No! Let's go." I head down the hallway.

Great. Now I'll have to wait another whole day to see how much Ollie hates me.

# CHAPTER 18

When Mr. Stein drops me off at home, Dad answers the door.

"Why aren't you at work?" I ask.

"I'm checking up on Mom. She went to the doctor again this morning, and her blood pressure was a little high. That's not good for the baby. She needs to rest for five days until her next appointment."

My heart sinks. The baby is stressed. Mom is stressed. We're the family-sized bucket of stress. "But is she okay?"

"She's fine." He pats me on the back.

I walk into the family room, where Mom's lying on the couch watching a cooking show. There's a bowl of popcorn and a full glass of lemonade in front of her.

"Mom, Dad said you were on bed rest!" I put my hands on my hips.

"I am. That's why I'm parked in front of the TV."

"But whenever I'm sick, you tell me I can't watch too much TV." Not to mention that she never lets me eat a whole bowl of popcorn on my own.

"I'm an adult, and this is a different kind of sick."

"It's for the baby," Dad adds.

"That's so unfair!" I burst out. "The baby gets to watch TV when it's sick, and I don't!" I stomp toward the kitchen.

Dad follows me. "What's gotten into you? Mom has to rest, and your behavior's not helping."

I sigh. "Sorry." I open the fridge and pull out the milk for a bowl of cereal.

"Rough day, *sheyne meydl*?" Dad sits down next to me at the kitchen table.

"Yeah. This boy thought I said something rude, but he misunderstood me."

I'm not even going to tell him about the trip to the nurse's office. The last thing I want Dad to do is check in with the nurse.

"Did you tell him that?" Dad asks.

"I tried, but then the class ended, and we left."

Dad nods. "That's tough. Tell you what—I need to get back to work, but how about Monty's tonight, just you and me?"

"Okay." I nod. No matter what, I'm never going to turn down cake-batter ice cream with gummy bears and sprinkles!

"That's my girl. We'll talk this evening." He fluffs my hair and goes back to the family room to say goodbye to Mom.

I try to finish my cereal, but I'm not that hungry, so I join Mom on the couch. "Sorry for snapping at you," I mumble.

She puts her arm around me. "Don't worry about it, Syd. Want to make it up to me by keeping me company?"

"Sure." Even though I'm still annoyed at her for all the embarrassing things she's done to me this summer, I love spending time with Mom.

I get her to change the channel to a bloopers show where people make funny mistakes on TV and movie sets. If there'd been a camera in our class today, everyone would've laughed when I said I didn't like Ollie. Then the director would've yelled "Cut!" and we would've done the scene again. The second time, I would've said, "Of course I like Ollie. He's my friend." No one would've laughed, not even Hailey, and then the director would've yelled, "That's a wrap!" and told us what a wonderful job we did. Too

142

bad this is real life and not a TV set.

It's nice to hang out with Mom, though. It feels like the way things used to be before she was pregnant. When the baby comes, she'll be so busy changing poopy diapers and cleaning up toys that we won't be able to lounge on the couch together.

Mom's cell phone rings. It's her friend Sandy, checking on her. A second later, the landline phone rings too, and Mom tells Sandy to hold on while she answers it. She says, "Hi, Maggie. Sydney would like you to come over." She says goodbye before I can react and goes back to Sandy.

"Mom, are you sure it's okay if Maggie comes over? I mean, you're supposed to be resting."

She lowers her phone while she responds. "Maggie's a boisterous girl, but as long as you guys aren't going to beat on my pots and pans, it'll be fine." She laughs.

I laugh too. In third grade, Maggie really wanted to play the drums, and she would walk around everywhere with drumsticks. Her dad had taken her to see a steel drum band, and she was convinced we could duplicate the sound with pots and pans. We had a lot of fun but ended up with huge headaches.

Barely five minutes later, Maggie and I are hanging out in my room. Once I've told her everything that happened in class and the nurse's office, I ask her what she thinks.

She's sprawled out on my bed, her feet hanging off the edge. "Ollie has already forgotten about what you said," Maggie says with a straight face. "He's forgotten about it because his parents are taking him on a surprise cruise for the rest of the summer."

I picture Ollie boarding a ship, carrying a huge suitcase, everything neatly folded and organized inside. "Good riddance, Margaret (Sydney)!" he shouts. I close my eyes and try to block out that image of Ollie running away.

"That doesn't make any sense," I say.

"I know." She slides off the bed and flops down onto the floor next to me. "Do you think I was really going to say something bad? I'm sure he just needs some time to cool off. It was just a misunderstanding."

"I guess."

The last misunderstanding I had was with my friend Lily at the beginning of the school year, and we didn't speak for three whole days. It was about the dumbest thing too. We were at lunch, and I pointed to the last brownie bite on her plate and said, "You going to eat that?" She thought I meant that she ate too much. She broke down crying. It took me a while to even understand what she thought I'd been implying. Well, she still didn't believe me when I said I hadn't meant it that way at all. Lily ended up stuffing the last brownie bite into her mouth anyway, and she refused to talk to me until Maggie finally staged an intervention.

"And I still can't believe you pulled off a trip to the nurse's office as *me*!" Maggie says. "It's pretty epic."

"I was freaking out. She was *this* close to calling your mom." I hold up my pointer finger and thumb an inch apart from each other.

"I'm impressed." Maggie smiles. "So, are you ready to go see Warren?"

"What?" I jump up. "When did we say we were going to visit him?"

"Um, I was thinking we need to do something to get your mind off Ollie."

I laugh. "Do you *like* like Warren?"

She sticks her hands in her pocket and rocks backward. "I don't know. I mean, I think I do. Is there a way to be sure?"

"I don't know much about this stuff. Do you think about him all the time?"

"Well, I think about a lot of things all the time. Warren, pizza, my dog, swimming, dance . . ."

"Ahem." I point to myself.

"And you, of course, Frankelstein!"

"Thanks. Okay, next question. Does your heart go *boom, boom, boom* when you see the Warrenster?" I slap my chest to add sound effects.

"No comment." She rolls her eyes at me. "Can we go now?"

"Sure. But I can't stay too long because my dad's taking me out for ice cream when he gets home."

"Warren, baby, here I come!" Maggie shimmies down the stairs.

"You're hopeless!" I trail after her.

I tell Mom we'll be back, and we head up the street to Warren's house.

On the way over, Mr. Smith pulls out of his driveway and rolls down his window. "Hi, Sydney."

"Hi." I stand there slightly frozen. He's shaved his beard. He looks a lot younger without it.

"Haven't seen your parents lately. How's your mom doing?" he asks.

"She's fine—resting."

"Good. Tell her to stop by for some gardenias if she's not bothered by the smell."

"The smell?" Maggie wrinkles her nose.

"They're strong-smelling flowers, and some pregnant women are very sensitive to smells. Mrs. Smith was." Mr. Smith belly laughs.

"Okay, thanks." I wave as he drives away. I turn to Maggie. "I used to be really scared of him."

"Why?"

"He had a thick grizzly beard and that deep laugh."

Maggie pulls a curl from each side of her head toward her nose and deepens her voice. "Do I scare you?"

I try the belly laugh, but all I get is a stomach cramp.

Maggie drops her hair and rings the doorbell. She stands on her tippy-toes and tries to peek through the small windowpanes on the door.

The door flies open. "What do you want?" Jake asks.

Maggie's mouth drops. "What are you doing here?"

"The question is, what are *you* doing here?"

"We came to see Warren," Maggie says.

"But seriously, why is Jake here?" I whisper.

"I heard that, Sydney." He laughs.

We follow him in, and he disappears upstairs with Mark, Warren's brother. We call after them to ask where Warren is, but they just shrug. So now we're standing in the middle of Warren's empty family room like lost puppies.

"Maybe we should go back outside and re-ring the doorbell," I suggest.

Maggie shakes her head. "And risk Jake answering again? Let's look around and see if we can find Warren ourselves." She pokes her head into the kitchen. "Not there."

"When I was here with my mom, Warren was in the garage."

"Good idea." She opens the heavy door, but no one's there. We don't see anything except a workout bench and a bunch of boxes.

"He's probably upstairs," I say. "And I don't want to go up to his bedroom."

"What about that room?" Maggie points to a half-open door at the end of the hall.

"I think that's the office." We take a few steps forward. "Yeah, it's him talking."

We both put our fingers to our lips and tiptoe forward. He's sitting at a desk with his back to us, and he looks like he's talking to the computer. We're a few inches from the door when I hear Warren say, "They're not cute."

Someone on the computer makes an *aww* noise.

"Crazy Hair grosses me out. And Big Ears—that name fits her!" Warren laughs.

Maggie and I stare at each other. We don't speak. He's talking about us.

My heart races. How could he be so mean?

I strain to hear what the other person is saying, but Warren's making a hissing sound. "They should be fed to the snakes!"

"You're too cruel, bro!" I hear the other voice say. "But Crazy Hair really likes you, so what are you going to do?"

"Tell Big Ears to keep her away from me!" Warren cracks up again.

Maggie's sniffling. I know she's trying hard to hold it all in.

"Let's go." I pull her arm.

She nods, and we let ourselves out, making sure the door slams behind us.

"We should be *fed to snakes*? Who says something

like that?" Maggie trudges down the street, her face turned toward the pavement.

I link arms with her. Ollie thinks I'm mean. Warren thinks we're ugly. This is officially the worst day ever.

We walk at a zombie pace toward my house. All of a sudden, though, Maggie lets go of my arm and pulls away from me. "You told him, didn't you?"

"Told him what?"

"That I liked him."

"No! Why would I do that? Oh . . ." I look down at my shoes. Why did I ever ask if they kissed at the movies? So stupid. I should've looked at the caller ID first.

She stamps her foot. "I can see it on your face! I know you said something."

"Calm down!"

"Calm down? How can I calm down? It's obvious I'm Crazy Hair and you're Big Ears." She pulls at her hair.

"I'm not Big Ears!" I say, even though being Crazy Hair wouldn't feel any better.

"Of course you are! And it's all your fault that Warren thinks I'm gross." She breaks down crying.

"I didn't mean to say anything!"

"Wait, so you *did* tell him? I knew it! You've ruined my life!" She turns around and runs the other way, toward her house.

I yell, "Wait!" But she doesn't look back.

## CHAPTER 19

I run into my house, pulling out the elastic from my ponytail so that my hair falls down and covers my ears. I may never wear my hair up again, thanks to Warren.

All I want to do is live the life of a groundhog. Then I could burrow deep underground and never come out. The downside is that I'd have to eat grasshoppers and snails, but I'm sure I could get used to it. For now, I'll settle for hiding in bed under my covers.

But before I can get to my room, I run into Dad in the kitchen.

"Ready for some ice cream, *sheyne meydl*?" Dad asks.

Oh, I totally forgot. "Before dinner?"

"Yeah, sure. Don't tell your mother, though." He chuckles.

"I heard that," Mom calls from the family room.

"I don't think so, Dad. I've lost my appetite."
I run up the stairs, holding in my tears just long
enough for them and me to crash onto my bed. Who
can eat ice cream at a time like this?

A minute later, I hear a soft knock on my door.
"Can I come in?" Dad asks.

"Yes," I whimper.

"Are you still upset about what happened with
the boy in your class?"

Ollie! I totally forgot he hates me too. More tears
escape from my eyes. "Yeah."

Dad sits down next to me. "Anything else bothering you?"

"Uh-huh," I say.

"Mom?" he asks.

Oh, geez, now I feel even guiltier. I wasn't
thinking about Mom and the baby either. I'm so self-
ish. "Yes. I don't want to give Mom more stress."
I sniffle.

Dad rubs my back. "It's okay. You can still talk to
us when you're upset."

"Thanks, Dad. It's just that Maggie's mad at me,
and . . . can I ask you one thing?" I reluctantly pull
my hair back. "Do I have big ears?"

"They're just like mine. Perfect."

I was afraid he'd say that. I press my hair against my ears. I'll never be able to play a sport where you have to wear your hair off your face. And what if I want to work in a restaurant? I'll get fired when I refuse to put my hair back and a stray hair ends up in a customer's soup. I'm doomed.

Dad stands up. "Come on. Let's go share a sundae." He holds out his hand and helps me off my bed.

"Okay, I'm coming." I'm already miserable, so I might as well be miserable with a bowl of my favorite ice cream.

Mom tells us to bring her home a double scoop of butter pecan, which is my twelfth-favorite ice cream out of the twenty-four flavors at Monty's. Halfway isn't too bad. Dad and I love Monty's because it's old-fashioned looking, and we always sit on the red swivel stools at the counter.

As we share our sundae, Dad tells me old stories about when he was a little boy. I've heard them before, but they're stories I love. About the time when he found a sick baby duck and brought it home. About the time he took a bite of a cake that Bubbe made for a dinner party and then tried to patch up the cake. And my favorite, about the time he got his foot stuck in his sister's volcano science project and was afraid it would erupt on him. Dad's stories are comforting, like my old plaid quilt that Mom made me stuff in the back of my closet after she got me a pink, puffy one.

I point to a glass jar next to the napkin dispenser that has a sign taped onto it. *If your service was dandy, tip's are appreciated.* "Look, Dad. They have a grammatical error. It's supposed to be *tips* without the apostrophe!"

He puts his arm around my shoulder. "*Sheyne meydl,* you're most certainly your mother's daughter."

I look down at my bowl. Swirls of hot fudge and clumps of bananas are swimming in the melted ice cream. "Do you think Mom will ever get over the county spelling bee? I know she was really disappointed that I decided not to go."

"Oh, Sydney," he says, "we're not disappointed in you. We just don't want you to make decisions based on fear. You're good at spelling, and you enjoy it. We don't want anything to hold you back from shining."

"I know." I sigh. I do enjoy practicing spelling words on my own. But I hate the pressure of other people watching me while I compete.

Dad cups his hand under his chin. "Let's say you

did go to the county competition. What would've made the event perfect?"

"Me winning." I grin. "I guess I couldn't just walk in there and automatically win, but it would've been cool to get one word right after another. And I've seen the gold trophies—they're huge. I would've put mine on top of my bookcase."

Dad doesn't move, like he's in deep thought. "Now, what's the worst thing that could've happened?"

"Hmm . . . . I could've peed my pants onstage."

"Really?"

"Nah, not really. But I could've gotten nervous and been gasping for air. Then my face would've gone bright red, and I wouldn't have been able to get any words out."

"And if you'd been able to control your nerves, then what would've been the worst thing?"

I shrug. "Getting eliminated on the first round and going back to school as a loser."

"A loser? Says who? Did anyone else win the school bee? No. You were a winner before the county bee even happened."

I run Dad's words over in my head. "You've got a point there."

"Thanks. I like to think I still have something left inside my coconut." He taps his head.

Dad's such a goof, but he makes me laugh.

"And on a more serious note," he continues, "it's all about preparation. If you think about what you're going to do, you'll be a lot more relaxed. Whenever I have to give a presentation for work, I make sure I know exactly what I'm going to talk about."

"But what if it's not a presentation? What if it's something else?" I'm thinking about Maggie, Ollie, and Warren.

"Well, I can't predict the future, but I do try to imagine the best and worst things that could happen. I think about what I want to get out of the meeting no matter how it goes. Most important, I'm always honest with myself." Dad looks me straight in the eye. I blink. "Does that help?"

"Yes. A lot." I can do that. I just want my friends back.

We eat until our bellies ache, and for a while, I forget about my terrible day. Of course, as soon as I get home, I think about Maggie all over again. About how she thinks I said all those awful things to Warren. I want to fix things between us, but I'm not going to apologize for something I didn't do.

## CHAPTER 20

As soon as I walk downstairs for breakfast, I'm blinded by the word of the day. Mom's bought some new neon markers, and the word *gumption* is in bright orange.

I've never heard that word before, so I read the definition under it: *having the nerve to do something others might not want to do.*

"I like that word," I tell Mom.

"It's a funny word, but it's important. People need gumption to make it in this world." She pulls out a box of cereal.

"I'm just trying to make it to sixth grade, Mom." My first step will be to use my gumption and apologize to Ollie again in class. Next, I'll call Warren and tell him what a jerk he is, and if I have any gumption left after that, I'll call Maggie and tell her she has things all wrong.

"I have a surprise that will make you happy." Mom pours me a glass of fresh-squeezed orange juice.

"What?" *You waved a magic wand and undid yesterday?*

"You can skip class today and hang out with me. Mr. Stein called to say Maggie is sick, so he won't be taking her to the community center, and I can't drive for a few days."

Sure, Maggie is sick. Sick of me.

"Nah, I want to go," I say. "Can Dad drive me?"

"I thought you'd be thrilled to hear this."

"Well, I, uh, I actually really want to go to class."

"Wow, that's a big change." Mom rubs her belly. "I'm sorry, though, because Dad has a big meeting today, so he can't take you either."

"This isn't happening!" I drop my spoon onto the tile floor. It makes a loud *clink*.

"Sydney, it's only one class. I'd drive you myself, but your father wouldn't be happy, nor would Dr. Fine."

"Mom, forget it." I push my chair back from the table and pick up my spoon. "Can I be excused? I want to go back to my room."

"Sure thing. Is everything okay?"

*No, not at all,* I want to shout. Everybody hates me—my best friend, our neighbor, and even the nicest kid in my class.

I think about what Dad said. About how Mom's on bed rest and any stress could harm her and the baby. "Everything's fine. I just feel like lying down for a few minutes."

"Okay. Call me if you need anything."

"I will." Not. I run upstairs and do a belly flop onto my bed. I stare at the row of honor roll certificates taped up on the wall next to my desk. Why did I ever put those up? They look stupid. I sink down into my comforter so I can't see them—or anything else, for that matter. I'm in a dark cave where nothing can bother me.

I wonder what Maggie's doing now. I picture her crying her eyes out while looking at one of our Frankelstein photo albums. And then I picture her tearing pictures of me into little itty-bitty pieces and feeding them to her dog. Well, she wouldn't do that, because she loves her dog, but she would feed them to her garbage can.

After ten minutes under the covers, I'm so bored—not to mention hot. I'm glad I have my iPad up here because at least I can kill some zombies. Even though I love playing these games, I don't see how Maggie's brother and his friends can play Xbox for hours and hours. Mom would say, "A person with gumption doesn't sit around all day playing video games. They make things happen."

But how do you make things happen when so much seems to be going wrong? I would ask Mom, but I don't want to bother her, and Maggie's out of the question now. Argh. I squeeze my pillow so hard that I'm afraid the stuffing is going to pop out. Maggie and I have been friends for six years, and this is our first real fight. Sure, we've been annoyed with each other here and there, but nothing major. This seems a lot more serious, because we haven't spoken for almost twenty hours. That's like a year in Frankelstein time.

I hear Mom's footsteps coming toward my room. She's breathing a little heavily. I jump out of my bed and race to my door. "Mom, are you okay?"

"Yes, I'm fine. I just wanted to tell you to hurry up and get ready because Mrs. Pendler is going to swing by in a few minutes. I asked her if she could take you to class. Then Dad can pick you up after his meeting."

"Really?" My heart does a running leap into my throat.

"Mrs. Pendler said it'll be no trouble to drop you off. The community center actually is on the way to Warren's basketball practice."

"Warren will be in the car?" I gasp.

"Yes. I thought you liked him now."

"For like a minute," I grumble. "But it turns out he thinks I have big ears."

"Since when?" Mom pulls back my hair. "Your ears are fine. Like Dad's."

"I know." I frown. "He already told me that."

"They suit your face beautifully," Mom says.

I run over to my mirror. "Now I have a big *face* too?"

"Sydney, what's gotten into you?"

Before I'm forced to answer her, a car horn beeps outside.

"Oh, that's your ride," Mom says.

I grab my bag. "Okay, thanks. I'm going."

"We'll talk more when you get back, all right?"

"Sure. Get some rest," I say as I run down the stairs.

As soon as I set foot out the front door, Mrs. Pendler rolls down her window and calls out to me. "Hello, Sydney! Hop in."

I thank her and pull open the back passenger door. Warren's sitting behind the driver's seat playing on his cell phone. Even Warren has a phone. So unfair.

I buckle up, and Mrs. Pendler pulls out of our driveway. We drive by Maggie's street. I wonder what she's doing today. And if she'll call me later.

"Has your mother been resting?" Mrs. Pendler asks.

"Yes, but I think she's getting bored," I say.

"I bet she is. It's important, though. She shouldn't be doing anything overwhelming, because stress can take a big toll on the body." Mrs. Pendler taps the steering wheel.

Yeah, like worrying about her eleven-year-old daughter, who is currently friendless. Good thing I didn't tell Mom about how my life stinks right now, or I would've sent her straight to the doctor with ridiculously high blood pressure.

Mrs. Pendler looks into the driver's mirror. "Warren, put the game away now. We have a guest in the car."

"It's okay," I say. "We're almost at the community center anyway." Besides, I have nothing nice to say to Warren, the cruelest boy on Earth.

Warren looks up. "Sorry. I got stuck on level 21."

He's smiling at me like nothing's wrong. I realize he doesn't know we were in his house yesterday. I should speak up about it, but I know that now, trapped in a car with his mom, is probably not the best time.

We pull up to the big light. Only two more minutes, and we'll be there. That's nothing when you compare it to how long I haven't spoken to Maggie.

Mrs. Pendler jabbers about babies until we pull up to the community center. It's one of those days when I'm happy to hear an adult blab so I don't have to talk.

When we reach the front of the building, Warren says, "Maybe I'll see you and Maggie later."

"Yeah, maybe," I answer as I get out of the car. I quickly thank Mrs. Pendler for the ride and run inside.

I'm a few minutes early, which is fine with me. Mrs. Wrigley's not in the room yet, but the door is open. I take my usual seat. Mary walks in first with her mother. I say hi, her mother says hi back, and Mary just nods. By the time her mom is out the door, Mary's already reading *Wonder*.

Sara walks in next. "Hi, Sara," I say. "How's your cat doing?"

"Bet-ter to-day. I feel bet-ter too."

"That's great." I can't tell that she's feeling any different by looking at her, but I guess she probably can't tell from looking at me that I feel ready to explode from nerves.

Finally, Ollie walks in. My heart thumps, and I swallow hard. I can do this. It's now or never. It doesn't matter if I'm nervous to talk to him; I need to apologize. "Ollie, I'm so sorry about what I said yesterday. I didn't mean it. I was just nervous. You're my friend! Please forgive me."

He sets his bag down next to me but doesn't say anything. My heart beats a little faster. What if he never answers?

"Please, Ollie. I'll do anything."

"Anything?" He laughs.

"Yes."

"Will you watch Mr. Toad for me while I'm away next weekend? Last time we were out of town, my neighbor Jack watched him. I don't think he spent much time with Mr. Toad, because Mr. Toad was sad when I got home, and he'd hardly eaten any of his food. This time, Jack's in Arizona, so that's not even an option."

I clap my hands. "Really? Of course! I'd love to

take care of Mr. Toad. I was afraid you hated me."

Ollie wipes a stray hair away from his face. "No, I'm fine. I thought about it, and know you didn't mean anything bad."

"Phew, because I felt terrible. I kept wishing I'd explained myself better."

"Then why didn't you call me?" He pulls out a canvas pouch and takes out three pencils.

"I thought you might hang up on me."

He stares at me for a second. "Do I look like the hanging-up type?"

"No, but what does the hanging-up type look like anyway?"

He squints his eyes and lets out a wimpy growl.

I laugh. "Ollie Moore, you couldn't play the mean guy in a movie even if you tried!"

"Oh yeah?" He straightens his back. "Let's see what you've got!"

I twist my lips back and forth, narrow my eyes, and let out a scoff.

Mrs. Wrigley enters the room, and her eyes bug out at me. "Everything all right?"

I freeze. I realize that Mary's staring straight at me. I wonder if she's been watching us this whole time.

"We were just having a growling contest," Ollie says.

"I see." Mrs. Wrigley sets her coffee cup on her desk. Sara, Alice, and Calvin all walk in and head for their seats.

"Thanks," I whisper to Ollie.

He gives me the thumbs-up. "Anytime."

I hold my hands up to my cheeks and realize they're not hot. I know they're probably a little pink, but that's definitely an improvement over being a ball of fire.

Mrs. Wrigley asks us to help her move all the chairs into a circle today because we're going to do a sharing exercise about the book.

"I didn't bring anything for show-and-tell," Calvin says.

"Don't worry. You weren't supposed to bring anything." Mrs. Wrigley starts forming the circle. "This is an exercise where we express our thoughts on the chapters we read."

When we're done moving the chairs, we sit down. Now I have Ollie on my left and Mary on my right.

"It's circle day," Calvin says to Hailey when she walks in.

"I can see that." She puts her hands on her hips and turns to Mrs. Wrigley. "This is weird."

"Always good to try something new." Mrs. Wrigley points to an empty seat.

Hailey plunks down in a chair on the other side of Mary. "But we're, like, right up in people's faces."

"That's also a good thing," Mrs. Wrigley says. "If you want to get to know people better, it helps to look at them when you talk."

I turn to Ollie. "Hi, Ollie. How are you?"

"I'm fine." He laughs.

It's good to be back to normal with him. I'm happy for a split second—until I think about Maggie and Warren. I can't believe Warren has ruined my friendship with Maggie.

"Before we start chatting about *Wonder*, let's go around and say something nice about each person. A word, a phrase, or a sentence. Who would like to be talked about first?"

"Me!" Hailey shouts. That's no surprise. She'd have her own reality show if someone offered it to her.

"Okay, I'll start," Mrs. Wrigley says. "Hailey's enthusiastic. She's always ready to get involved."

"I think she means *take over*," Ollie whispers in my ear. He's so right!

"Hailey has nice hair," Calvin says, even though it's not his turn to comment yet.

"She's interesting and always has a lot of stories," I say when they get to me.

This is actually pretty easy—and fun too. I have something to say about everyone except for Mary. She never talks, so we don't know very much about her.

Sara says that Mary's a thinking machine. Which is kind of funny because Sara *sounds* like a machine. I end up saying Mary is sweet. She doesn't look at us much, but when she does, it's with kind eyes.

Ollie's next. My heart beats fast again. I don't want to say anything embarrassing, but I want to say something special. Hailey says he's nice, and Mrs. Wrigley says he's thoughtful. I'm the last one to go.

I look over at Ollie. I think about how his bag is full of things people might need and about how he gave the lollipop to Sara when she was sad. I think about how he tried the electric scooter even though he knew it would be hard for him.

"The thing I like most about Ollie is that he has gumption."

Mrs. Wrigley's eyes go wide. "I haven't heard anyone in my class use that word before. Splendid word."

"What does *gum-shun* mean?" Sara asks.

"Do you want to explain, Margaret?" Mrs. Wrigley says.

"It's when someone knows what they want and goes for it. Nothing holds them back," I say.

"Perfect! I hope all of you in here are learning to use your gumption to go for the things you want and not be held back by fears or self-doubts."

"Amen!" Calvin shouts.

"We're not in church," Hailey scolds him.

Everyone's quick to say nice things about Ollie. I hope they're as kind to me.

"Okay, let's move on to Margaret," Mrs. Wrigley says.

I feel my face getting red again. Deep breath in. Deep breath out. I try my best to control it. I wait for someone to yell something silly, but nobody does.

Calvin makes a bunch of *ooo-ooo* noises and raises his hand to go first. "Margaret is spunky!"

Mrs. Wrigley says that's a great description. I like being called spunky. Sara calls me a good girl, and Mary writes on her piece of paper that I'm friendly.

Alice says I'm a kindred spirit, which I think means I'm like her.

Mrs. Wrigley glances over to Hailey, who's playing with her sparkly pink pen. "Oh, I'm next?" she asks.

Mrs. Wrigley nods.

I hold my breath.

"Margaret . . ." She draws out my (Maggie's) name. " . . . is very normal."

I exhale. I'll take it.

Ollie holds up a pen with a light on the end. He switches it on. "Margaret is a spark."

"Spark?" Hailey questions.

"The spark in the room. You know, the light that shines."

"Yes, I get it," Hailey cuts him off.

"Thanks," I whisper. That's the sweetest thing anyone besides my parents has said about me. My heart is warm.

"I agree. Margaret's a dynamo," Mrs. Wrigley adds.

*Dynamo.* That's a cool word. Mom would love it. I could get used to all of this sharing. I may be a little red, but this is a happy red.

Once we're done with everyone, Mrs. Wrigley

asks us what we think about Auggie from *Wonder*. When she gets to me, I say I don't see how people could be mean to him just because he looks different. She says she wished everyone thought that way. Me too.

Mrs. Wrigley has each person read a couple of paragraphs of the next chapter out loud. Sara goes really slowly, and Mary reads in a whisper, but no one says anything mean about them. Not even Hailey.

For the last five minutes, Mrs. Wrigley gives us time to chat. Ollie asks me a lot of questions about the baby. He says his older cousin had a baby a couple of months ago, and she's super cute. I know what he's saying—babies *are* cute. I just don't know what it's going to be like to have one at my house, full time, forever, no givesies backsies.

With the baby around, will Dad still have time to take me out for ice cream? Will Mom still cook amazing dinners for us, or will we have to eat Easy Mac every night?

"Have your parents picked any names yet?" Ollie asks.

"They said maybe Noah or Nicole. They'd like a name that starts with an *N* because my great-grandmother's name was Nancy. And the middle name will be Aubrey because both dad and I have *A* middle names."

"Cool. What's your middle name?" he asks.

"Ah, it's bad."

"Bad how?"

"Embarrassing. Do you have a middle name?"

"Cable."

"Ollie Cable. That's a cool name."

"It's my mom's maiden name. What's yours? Allison? Amy? Ashley?"

"None of the above."

"I'll figure it out." Ollie smiles.

"Be my guest." I fold my arms against my chest. There's no way he's going to guess it.

When Dad picks me up, I'm in a much better mood.

"How was class today?" he asks as I get into his car.

"Good. I patched things up with my friend."

"I'm glad to hear it. And how are things with Maggie?"

"Ah, I still haven't spoken to her."

He pulls into traffic just as the light turns yellow. "Sometimes you just have to take the plunge."

"Huh?"

"Be the first one to make a move. Give her a call."

"You make it sound simple." I think about how Maggie and I used to go to the pool here at the community center and how I'd always make her jump off the diving board first. I guess it's my turn to go first.

"It really is." He smiles into the mirror.

"Let me guess: I just have to be prepared."

"You're a fast learner, Sydney Frankel!"

When we get home, I grab the phone and go to my room for some privacy. I rehearse what I'm going to say, and then I dial Maggie's number before I have time to change my mind.

One ring . . . two rings . . . three rings . . . "What's up?"

Just as I feared: Jake.

"Hi, can I speak to Maggie?"

"Sydney, I thought you'd never call! Did you know that every year, more people are killed by vending machines than sharks?"

"No. That stinks. But can I speak to Maggie?" I pace up and down the room.

"Maggie? I thought you called to talk to *me*."

"Um, no. I called for Maggie."

"Really? Are you sure?"

"*Yes*."

He cackles. "I'm just kidding around with you, Sydney."

"Okay." It's hard to laugh when I'm nervous.

"Hate to break it to you, but Maggie's not home."

I slump down on my desk chair. "Can you tell her I called?"

"I'll try, but you know how fuzzy my brain is."

"I know," I say and hang up. I wonder where she is. And who knows if she'll ever get my message. This is awful.

I run upstairs. All I want to do is lie on my bed. It's so boring without Maggie talking my ear off. I feel like half of my soul is missing. It's hard to be the Frankel without the Stein.

Is it possible that this can be the best *and* worst day ever?

## CHAPTER 21

It's been forty-six hours since I've heard from Maggie. That's a lifetime in Frankelstein years. I'm trying not to let my parents see how upset I am, but it's hard. At this point, even my soon-to-be sibling can probably tell something is wrong.

Dad enters my bedroom with one hand behind his back. "I have something that will cheer you up."

I put down my book. "What is it? A cell phone?"

"Close. How about a kitchen phone?" He pulls the phone out from behind his back. "Maggie's on the other line."

"Yay!" I grab the phone from him.

Dad stands there with his arms crossed.

I smile. "Thanks for bringing it to me."

"You're welcome, *sheyne meydl*." Dad's still standing there, smiling.

I cover the mouthpiece with my hand. "Bye."

He winks and leaves me alone.

"Hi, Maggie?" I'm not sure if she's even still there.

"Syd, I called to, um—I'm sorry, all right?" She starts to cry.

"Don't cry, Maggie. It's okay. I'm sorry too." I breathe a sigh of relief. "I never told Warren that you liked him. But after you guys went to the movies, I picked up the phone and thought it was you. So the first thing I said was, 'Did you kiss?' As a joke, obviously, but—"

"Ahhh! That's so embarrassing! Way worse than when he heard me saying super-duper pooper-scooper!"

"Agreed," I sigh. "But I never meant for Warren to know that you liked him."

"Frankelstein, you're the best secret keeper. I shouldn't have jumped to conclusions. You don't hate me, do you?" Maggie asks.

"Of course not! That would be like hating myself, Frankelstein! Besides, I know you were upset with Warren, and that's why you blew up at me."

"Don't even say his name. Just call him Toad."

"Oh, can we please call him something else? Mr. Toad is the name of Ollie's turtle."

"Ollie has a turtle?" she asks.

"Yes, and he asked me to babysit it next weekend."

"For real? Okay. Then how about we call Warren Snake Boy?"

"Perfect. We should go talk to Snake Boy—let him know he was a big jerk."

"I don't want to. The damage is done." She sniffs.

I think back to the misunderstanding I had with Lily last year. Lily was so sure I was being mean to her when I honestly hadn't meant to hurt her feelings. "But what if it was a mistake?"

"Can't be," Maggie says. "We heard him loud and clear."

"But . . . he never used our actual names."

"Didn't need to."

"Okay, but maybe you should ask Jake if he heard anything." I catch a glimpse of my ear in the mirror. I pull my hair over it.

"You know Jake can't keep a secret."

"That's true." I have a quick flashback to when we were in second grade and Jake told everyone that Maggie and I had worn matching red footie Elmo pajamas to our sleepover. Everyone was laughing at us. It was not a pretty sight.

"It was a horrible two days without you, Frankelstein," Maggie groans.

"You too, Frankelstein. It was actually forty-six hours to be exact." I think about my talk with Dad. About how sometimes it's important to take the plunge. "Hey, do you want me to go over to Warren's with you?"

"No, I don't want to talk to him. At all."

"Fine. I'll banish his name from our vocabulary."

"Whose name?" Maggie laughs.

"Exactly."

Maggie and I stay on the phone for an hour. We talk about nothing and everything. I tell her about how I apologized to Ollie without turning red.

We finally get off the phone when my parents call me to dinner. Dad's made his special gourmet pizzas—the one food he's really good at cooking. My favorite is the tomato mushroom, and Mom loves the spinach and ricotta cheese.

"Sydney, I have an appointment with Dr. Fine in the morning," Mom says as soon as I walk into the kitchen. "Would you like to come with me?"

"Sure. Is Dad driving you?"

"No, I'll be fine."

Dad places the pizzas on the table and sits down.

"You know, I could sneak out of the conference early to take you."

"I've got it under control. I'm feeling great. Now cut me a slice of pizza before I faint." She laughs.

Dad and I both shake our heads at her before Dad slices the pizzas.

"Do you guys like turtles?" I ask a minute later, fully aware that I have cheese sticking to my chin.

"I've never eaten turtle pizza. I'd think it'd be too crunchy," Dad says.

"Gross! That's not funny." I pretend to gag.

"Turtles are used a lot in literature, in fables." Mom sprinkles Parmesan on her pizza slice.

I slap the table with my hand. "Great! Then you guys won't mind that Ollie asked me to babysit his turtle next weekend?"

Mom frowns. "Oh, I don't know about that."

"Aww, a cute little reptile," Dad says in a soft voice.

"I've heard they can carry salmonella," Mom points out.

My stomach drops.

"I don't think that would be a problem as long as Sydney makes sure to wash her hands after she handles the turtle," Dad says. "And as long as she keeps its tank extra clean."

Mom pauses and grits her teeth. "I suppose it'll be okay."

"Thanks so much!" I stand up and wrap my arms around her. Next, I walk over to Dad's side of the table and give him a big hug too.

"But you need to take care of it yourself," Mom says.

"I will, I will." I jump up and down.

Really, how hard can it be to watch a small turtle?

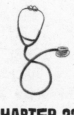

## CHAPTER 22

Mom says I'll be able to see the baby swimming around in her stomach at her doctor's appointment. I'm excited to find out more about the eggplant. If it's swimming slowly, then maybe it'll be a calm baby, but if it's doing a booty shake, then it could be one of those wild babies that destroys everything in sight. If that's the case, I'm asking for a lock on my bedroom door.

On the drive over, we talk about different baby name possibilities.

"If you don't go with a name that starts with *N*, I like Cleopatra," I say.

"Has a lot of spunk to it," Mom agrees.

I think about how Calvin said I was spunky. "Or what about Lancelot?"

Mom laughs. "The baby's going to be lucky to have you as a big sister."

I hope so.

We park right in front of the doctor's office, which is lucky, because it starts to rain as soon as we pull in. We rush inside the building and over to the elevator. The door opens and another *very* pregnant lady steps into the elevator with us. She looks like she swallowed a whole watermelon. I wonder if Mom will get that big.

A bunch of patients are spread throughout the large waiting room. Their stomachs are all different sizes. There are other kids here too, but most of them are toddlers. I'm going to be eleven and a half years older than the baby. I'll be in my last year of college when the baby starts middle school. I can take the baby to the movies, mini golfing, to the beach. We could have fun.

When Mom's name is called, she goes into a little room to have her blood pressure taken and get some blood drawn. Next, she has to go into the bathroom to leave a urine sample. I don't follow her there. After that, a nurse shows us to Room 4. Mom lies on the table, and I sit beside her.

After a few minutes, Dr. Fine enters and shakes my hand. She's a lot younger than I thought she'd be. She has Mom pull up her shirt, and she spreads clear gooey gel on Mom's stomach. It looks like slime.

Dr. Fine turns to me. "Sydney, I'm listening for the baby's heartbeat now. When I'm done, I'll print a picture for you to keep."

"Cool. How does the baby sound?"

We all hear the loud *thump, thump* through the machine.

Dr. Fine gives us the thumbs-up. "Now, if you take a look over at the sonogram machine, you'll be able to see the baby."

I jump up to take a closer look. The image is much clearer than the one I saw in the picture from Mom's last checkup.

Dr. Fine points to the machine. "Okay, there's the head . . . and the arms . . . and the legs." It looks like the baby's doing the backstroke. Not too fast. Not too slow.

I walk out of there with my very own black-and-white picture of my little sibling—so cool. I'm kind of glad that Mom and Dad don't want to find out the sex ahead of time. It'll be a neat surprise. Dr. Fine tells Mom that she needs to take it easy but that her blood pressure looks okay, so she's off bed rest.

When we get home, I park myself on the couch and stare at the picture of Cleopatra or Lancelot or the names Mom and Dad like, Nicole and Noah.

I wonder if the baby will be shy or goofy or loud. I wonder if they'll have gumption. I wonder if they'll grow as tall as me.

The phone rings and breaks me out of my daydreaming.

"I'll get it, Mom," I say and hop off the couch to check the caller ID. "Hi, Bubbe."

"Hello, Sydney! How's my *bubbelah* doing?"

"I'm good." I lean against the kitchen counter and stare at the word of the day. *Gratitude*. I definitely have gratitude for Bubbe and her love.

"How's the dance class? Are you ready to trade some moves with your old grandmother?" She chuckles.

There goes my guilt-o-meter. "Sure." I try to smile even though she can't see me.

"Okay, what's troubling you?"

Mom must've gotten her mind-reading powers from Bubbe. "Ah, it's nothing. Just that I heard a boy say something mean about me and Maggie, and I can't stop thinking about it."

Bubbe clicks her tongue. "Ack, what do those boys know?"

"But Maggie likes him."

"Well, then march over to his house and give him a piece of your mind!"

"Bubbe!" Mom always says she's feisty.

"It's best to talk things out. You've got nothing to lose."

"You're right," I admit. "Thanks."

I pass the phone to Mom and grab my shoes. I need to go to Warren's house and tell him that Maggie and I heard everything he said. I need to tell him it was wrong of him to talk like that. After all, Maggie's my best friend.

Mom's still talking to Bubbe. I tell her I'm going to Warren's. Her lips part as if she wants to ask why, but she doesn't. Which is good because I don't feel like explaining.

As I get closer to his house, my nerves kick in. What am I doing? I should run home now! What if Warren gets really mad that we eavesdropped on his private conversation?

I'm standing on his front steps, staring at the Pendlers' red curlicue welcome sign. I think about Dad's advice—to imagine the worst and best things that could happen. The worst: Warren could say that everything he said was the absolute truth and that he doesn't regret it. The best: He could apologize and mean it.

My finger hits the bell before my mind can stop

it. I count the seconds until someone comes. Twenty-eight, twenty-nine—right at thirty, the door opens. It's Mrs. Pendler. With her phone tucked under her ear, she gestures for me to come in and waves me toward the family room.

"Thank you," I whisper.

In the family room, Warren's watching TV with his feet up on the coffee table and a bowl of chips at his side. He's wearing his basketball uniform. From the doorway, he looks nice, not like a traitor.

I plunk down on the end of the couch and clear my throat.

He turns his head. "Hey, Sydney. I didn't see you come in."

"Just got here. Your mom let me in."

"Cool."

I take a deep breath. "Listen, I heard what you said about Maggie and me."

"Huh?" His eyebrows cling together like long-lost friends.

"You know."

"No, really, I don't."

I look down at my feet. "I had a feeling you'd say that. But we heard everything. We came to say hello on Monday, and Jake let us in. You were in the office talking to someone on the computer. You called me Big Ears and Maggie Crazy Hair. We thought we were your friends."

There! I said it without tripping over my words.

All of a sudden, Warren cracks up.

"Why are you laughing? You're such a jerk!" I squash the lump in my throat. I'm *not* going to cry.

"I'm laughing because I was talking to my friend Scott in Chicago. And he was showing me his new pet rats, Big Ears and Crazy Hair!"

"You had him name his rats after us?" I gasp.

Warren's laughing so hard that the couch is shaking. "Those are the names that *he* gave the rats. They have nothing to do with you or Maggie."

"Oh." My face is red hot. There might as well be a sign flashing over my head with an arrow pointing down that says *STUPID*. "But rats don't even have hair! They have fur."

"I know that, but Crazy Hair sounds better than Crazy Fur."

"True." This is definitely Phase 5 facial redness.

He stops laughing. "And why would you ever think I'd say something like that about you and Maggie?"

"Um . . ." I tuck a piece of hair behind my ear. "Because we heard you talking and because I have big ears."

"No, you don't. And Maggie has cool curly hair."

"Ugh. Sorry. I feel dumb. Rats, really?"

"Scott has all kinds of pets—dogs, a cat, lizards, a bunny, and now two rats."

"I can't believe Maggie and I had a fight over this," I mumble to myself. How ridiculous.

Warren gets up from the couch. "I have a basketball game today, but maybe we all can go to that ice cream place soon."

"Ice cream place?"

"Yeah, the Scooper Dooper. I heard they were back in business."

I freeze.

I know I'm turning redder.

Neither of us says anything.

Until Warren cracks up again.

"Okay, you got me," I say with a smile. "But if you want to go to a *real* ice cream place, Monty's is the best."

"Good to know," he says.

As soon as I get home, I call Maggie and ask to come over. When I get to her house, she rushes me inside and whispers, "I saw Jake and Olivia kissing, and now I can't unsee it."

"Gross!"

She makes kissy sounds to annoy me.

"Enough! I've got good news!"

"Tell me!" she squeals.

"Your room." Last thing we need is Jake and Olivia listening to our conversation since he's friends with Warren's brother.

In Maggie's room, I claim the beanbag while Maggie sits on her bed. I tell her, "I talked to Warren—"

"What? Why?" She throws her hands up in the air. "Did you tell him we think he's the meanest person on the planet?"

"No, but I did find out the truth. His friend in Chicago has two new pet rats, whose names just happen to be Big Ears and Crazy Hair."

Her mouth drops. "What? So . . . he wasn't talking about us?"

"Nope." I cross my legs under me. "We were mad at him for nothing."

She hits her chest with her hand. "Good! My heart didn't fail me. But I can't believe you went over and talked to him alone!"

"Me neither. And the best thing is I didn't hyperventilate or get stuck on my words. I got a little red,
but it wasn't that noticeable."

"That's great! I'm proud of you, Frankelstein!"

I'm proud of me too.

## CHAPTER 23

I can't believe it's been more than a month since we started classes at the community center. The days are moving a lot faster than I thought they would, and we only have three weeks left of the program.

Today, we've made it halfway through *Wonder*, and it's time for our sharing exercise. Mrs. Wrigley leans back against her desk. "We all have our differences—and similarities too. We're all here in this class for a reason."

"Yeah, because our parents signed us up," Hailey says.

"She does have a point," Alice agrees.

"That's true, but dig deeper," says Mrs. Wrigley. "There's a reason they thought each of you would benefit from this class."

"What made you want to teach this class, Mrs. Wrigley?" Ollie asks.

"Well, during the school year, I'm a middle school guidance counselor. Before that, I taught reading. Moving from elementary school to middle school is a huge transition, and being a comfortable reader makes everyone feel more secure."

"Do you work at Coral Rock Middle?" I ask.

"Yes, I do, along with two other counselors."

A flash of panic shoots through me. If Mrs. Wrigley's my school counselor next year, she's going to realize I'm not Margaret!

But by the time school starts, this summer program will be in the past. I can tell her the truth when I see her in the fall, and I bet she'll understand why I lied. Even if she doesn't, she'll probably be too busy with school stuff to rat me out to my parents.

"Anyone going to Coral Rock Middle this year?" She looks around the room.

I go ahead and raise my hand. So do Ollie, Hailey, Alice, and Mary. Hmm. I'm happy about Ollie being at my school, but Hailey? Not so much.

"Wonderful. I've been there for twenty-five years. I hope you'll love it there as much as I do."

"Wow, you're an old lady!" Calvin claps for her.

"Thanks, Calvin." She smiles. "Before I ask you all to share, I want to let you know that as a kid I was shy and definitely awkward." Mrs. Wrigley's glasses slide down the bridge of her nose, and she pushes them back up.

"Like me?" Calvin beams.

"You're not shy, doofus!" Hailey says.

"No, but I am awkward!" He pounds his chest. We all laugh.

"I am awk-ward too." Sara nods. "Aug-gie feels awk-ward in the book."

"He sure does," Mrs. Wrigley says. "Okay, who wants to share something that makes you feel different?"

Ollie raises his hand. "I feel different because of my dyspraxia. Before the doctors diagnosed me, my mom called me her clumsy little baby. And nobody ever wants me on their team in PE."

I gasp. Poor Ollie. That sounds so lonely. "I'm sorry."

"It's okay," he says. "I've had a lot of therapies, and I've gotten much better. It's just hard to play sports sometimes because I'm always afraid I'll fall and people will laugh at me. That's why I love to read so much. It's an escape."

"Ollie, thanks for being so open with the class," Mrs. Wrigley says. "That takes gumption." She winks at me and asks me to share next.

It takes me a minute to come up with what to say. "Something that makes me different is that when I speak in front of people, I turn all red and sound like I'm out of breath. That's why my mom made me take a class here. She thinks I need better self-esteem because I turned down a chance to go to the county spelling bee."

"That sounds awful!" says Alice. "Is that why you turned red and had to go to the nurse one day?"

"Yes." I nod.

"Have you ever passed out?" Calvin asks.

"No, I just have trouble catching my breath. Think like when you run a race and you have to breathe heavily."

"I hate running," Calvin declares.

"Thanks for sharing, Margaret," Mrs. Wrigley says. "I know that wasn't easy." Actually, it wasn't so bad. I feel comfortable with this group.

"Anything else you want to share before we move on?" Mrs. Wrigley asks me.

That I've been lying to her and everyone else in the class?

When I don't respond, Mrs. Wrigley says, "Sara, how about you?"

"The way I talk is diff-er-ent," Sara says. "Peo-ple laugh at me. I do not like it."

"Sara, I'm glad you're telling us how you feel. It's good to let it out," Mrs. Wrigley says.

"Peo-ple think I am str-ange. But I like me. And I like this class. You are my friends." Sara flashes a huge smile, as if someone's pulling a string from either side of her mouth. "My par-ents sent me here to make friends."

"I like this class too," Ollie agrees. "We're all friends."

"I have a lot of friends," Hailey says. "I mean, a real lot. So it's kind of hard to have more."

Mrs. Wrigley narrows her eyes at her. "You know, Hailey, the great thing about friends is that you can't really have too many of them. It's good to be open to making new ones, no matter how many we may have already."

"Fine. Sorry!" Hailey huffs.

"Would you like to share with the group about what makes you different?" Mrs. Wrigley asks her.

Hailey jumps out of her seat. "I'm *not* different! I don't have a problem, all right?" And with that, she races out the door. Mrs. Wrigley asks us to hold on for a moment and rushes after Hailey.

Geez, I wonder why she got so upset. I mean, I don't like being in front of groups or talking on the phone. I worry about silly little things, and I have a hard time standing up for myself. But lately, none of that feels as embarrassing or as impossible to deal with as it used to. I feel lucky to be me . . . even if, technically, this whole class thinks I'm Maggie.

The others start whispering, trying to figure out what's wrong with Hailey. I thought her life was perfect. Even though Mom says there's no such thing as perfect, I figured maybe Hailey was the exception.

"She could be an alien," Calvin suggests.

"That would be too obvious," I say.

"A spy." Ollie holds his finger to his lips and pretends to look around sneakily.

"Loudest spy ever," I say.

"She's just an immature, spoiled brat," Alice murmurs.

Ollie leans toward me. "Honestly, she's the only one in this class I have a hard time getting along with. I like everybody else a lot. That seems lucky, doesn't it? My mom told me this class could be boring because a lot of the students might be in here to improve their reading, not because they love to read. But it's worked out really well."

"I feel guilty being here," I admit. "I haven't been honest with people."

"Why? Is this still about your middle name?" He laughs. "Angelica? Astrid? Autumn?"

"No, none of those, and I'm not joking." I lower my head.

"Come on, you can tell me," he says quietly.

After I look around to make sure no one is listening, I lean over and whisper, "Um, my name isn't actually Margaret."

"Huh?"

I push my desk closer to his and speak as quietly as possible. "My name is Sydney Frankel. My mom actually signed me up for the dance combo class. My best friend, Margaret—nickname Maggie—was signed up for reading. So we decided to switch."

Ugh, I hope he doesn't hate me. But at the same time, it feels good to get that off my chest. To tell somebody I can trust.

Ollie's eyes light up. "Wow. You've got gumption, Sydney A. I mean, Margaret A."

"It's actually Margaret B. Thanks, but I feel guilty. My mom said I couldn't take reading because she wanted me to take a class that would help me get out of my shell."

"Well, has this class helped you do that?"

"It actually has!"

"I'm glad you're here. If you were in the other class, I wouldn't have made a new friend." Ollie looks down at his paper.

"Aw, thanks." I smile. "You're the best thing about this class."

Did I just say that? Maybe I'm turning into Maggie!

Mrs. Wrigley returns with Hailey, who sits back down.

"Whatever we say in here stays in here, right?" Hailey looks around to make sure we all agree. Mrs. Wrigley nods for her to continue.

"Okay. I'm different because, um, I make up stories." She picks at her cuticle. "I say stuff about my life that's not true."

She glances around the room again, but no one says anything. I'm in shock. I think everyone is.

"My mom's not pregnant. I have two brothers, but they're a lot older—twenty-two and twenty-four. I know I say a lot of things that sound exciting, but they're not true either. I was born here in Miami, and I've never ridden any animals. Not even a horse. My mom put me in this class because she wanted me to meet Mrs. Wrigley before I start middle school. I just wanted people to like me. And I failed." She puts her head down on the desk, her long hair covering her face like a veil.

This is so bizarre. I never would've guessed that Hailey was just as nervous about being here as I was. Now I know what adults mean when they say people can surprise you.

Mrs. Wrigley walks over to her and pats her on the shoulder. Without lifting her head, Hailey says, "I shouldn't have said anything. Now you all probably think I'm weird."

"No way." Ollie smiles. "You haven't seen my cousin Leo. Now, *he's* weird. The guy sucks down raw eggs for breakfast and once slept on a bed of nails."

"Cool," I say. "He sounds really interesting."

"See—what might be strange to one person is intriguing to another," Mrs. Wrigley says. "If you walk around with your eyes open, you'll learn a lot about people."

"Why would people walk around with their eyes closed?" Calvin asks.

Mrs. Wrigley laughs. "It's an expression, Calvin. It means they don't pay close attention to the world around them."

"Sil-ly peo-ple," Sara says.

Hailey raises her head. She looks like she's holding back tears. I actually feel sorry for her. I know she lied to us—a lot—but I also know that it's not easy to tell the truth all the time. With my big lie, I'm not much different from Hailey. Except my case *is* different, because Maggie and I were helping each other out. Right?

"I've lied before too," I blurt out.

I expect Mrs. Wrigley to ask me what lies I've told, but instead she asks, "What did you learn from that experience?"

"Um." I fidget with my pen cap. "Maybe . . . that I don't have to make stuff up when I feel nervous. And that things might not be as bad as I think they are."

"Yes, that's always good to keep in mind." Mrs. Wrigley doesn't move her eyes away from me. "Hiding the truth and running away from our problems will rarely work for long. We have to face our fears."

I wonder if that's what Dad meant when he said that he and Mom didn't want me to make decisions based on fear.

"You are a ver-y smart la-dy." Sara rocks back and forth in her chair.

"Thanks, Sara," says Mrs. Wrigley. "These are things you learn as you get older. One thing to remember is that everyone has fears and insecurities. We often don't know what kinds of burdens other people have. Think about Auggie in *Wonder*. Try to be kind to the people around you."

I look over at Hailey. She's quietly sitting at her desk. She hasn't moved an inch. I know she's embarrassed inside and out. I really do feel bad for her.

## CHAPTER 24

When Mom picks us up, she asks Maggie and me what we like best about our classes. I say the teacher and the other students, which isn't technically lying. Maggie says, "I like the book we're reading. It's called *Wonder*." She manages to talk about the plot for the whole ride home, which is impressive. She must actually be reading the copy I loaned her.

Maggie has lunch with us since both her parents are busy this afternoon. A few minutes after we finish eating and head up to my room, Mom comes in. "Warren's on the phone."

"Thanks." I take it from her and cover the mouthpiece. "Do you want to talk to him, Maggie?"

She shakes her head. "No, he called you."

"Hi, Warren."

"Hi, Sydney. Do you and Maggie want to go for ice cream at five?"

"Hold on, let me see if Maggie's free."

Maggie nods and mouths a big *yes*.

"Okay, we're in."

"Cool. We'll pick you guys up then," Warren says and hangs up.

"He's nice," I remark to Maggie.

"Now you know why I like him."

"Well, I like him too, but you *like* like him."

"I know." Maggie starts singing. "*Oh, Warren, Warren, you're so cute. Your hair is brown and spiky, and your eyes are swimming-pool blue . . .*"

"Uh, Maggie, I think it might be a good idea to keep that song to yourself."

"What are you saying? That I'm not a singing sensation?" She pretends to be offended.

"No, but you might want to save your talent for the middle school talent show."

"There's a talent show? Seriously?"

"Yes, my mom told me about it last year."

"Cool," she squeals. "Want to do a duet?"

I think about being on a huge stage with all the eyes in the audience staring at me, waiting for me to belt out a tune. Sure, Maggie will be next to me, but it's not as if I can hide behind her. I'm six inches taller.

"I'll think about it," I say.

At five, when we get into Mrs. Pendler's car, Warren says, "I haven't been to Monty's in so long. But I heard from a very reliable source that they've still got the best ice cream around." He winks at me.

"And Sydney and I know all the flavors," says Maggie. "We can list them for you now if you need extra time to consider your options."

Warren grins. "Do you work there or something?"

"I would if I could, but you have to be sixteen," she says. "I already asked."

"My cousin used to work at an ice cream place, but then she said her arm got too tired from scooping," Warren says. "She plays the violin, and it was messing up her practicing."

Maggie and I both move our hands back and forth like we're scooping.

"Looks like you guys are playing air guitar." Warren laughs.

"Perfect! That'll be our talent for the middle school talent show!" Maggie shouts.

"No way," I snort.

"I'm in." Warren turns around and high-fives her.

I'm glad he moved back to the neighborhood.

**CHAPTER 25**

Mom swishes into the kitchen wearing a flowy, red shirt.

"That's pretty," I say from my seat at the table. "Did you just get it?"

"I had to. I'm bursting out of everything else."

Her stomach does seem to be approaching basketball size. "Do you think the baby will eventually be as tall as me?"

"I wouldn't be surprised. There are a lot of tall people on both sides of our family if you go back far enough." She points to a photo of Dad's bubbe on the kitchen windowsill. She towers over her sisters in the picture.

"Was I tall when I was born?"

Mom smiles. "Both the nurse and the doctor commented on how long your legs were. And I always had to cut the feet off your pajamas when you were small."

"Oh, great. I was Bigfoot even back then." I sigh.

"You have beautiful feet."

Well, I hope they stop growing soon, or I'll have to share shoes with Dad. "Thanks, Mom. Okay, don't forget I'm bringing Mr. Toad home after class today."

"A toad? I thought it was a turtle."

"It is. Ollie named his turtle Mr. Toad."

"I think I need to meet this Ollie. He seems like quite a character."

"He is, Mom. He's super nice, and he gets me."

"Ah." She smiles knowingly.

I put my hands on my hips. "What?"

"Nothing." But after a couple of seconds, she says, "Okay, fine, I'll say it. You wouldn't have met him if you'd sat around at home all summer."

She has me there. "True."

Mom's phone buzzes. She steps toward the counter to pick it up, then grabs the edge of the counter instead. "Maggie's dad is on his way," she says casually, looking at the phone screen. "And Maggie's riding home with him after class because they're having lunch with relatives. So it'll be you and me and Mr. Toad on the way back."

I notice she's still leaning on the counter to steady herself. "Are you feeling okay?"

"Yes, just a little dizzy. Happens sometimes when I'm hungry." She grabs a yogurt from the fridge, sits down at the table, and digs in.

I grab a chocolate chip granola bar off the counter. "Do you want one of these too?"

"No, thanks. I'm feeling better now."

I kiss Mom goodbye and head out the door. I hope she's going to be okay.

*  *  *

When I walk into class, Mary is sitting alone in her usual corner spot. "Hi, Mary," I say and slide into my seat.

She nods at me and whispers, "Hi."

I do a double take. Wow, she actually said something to me. I mean, I couldn't really hear her, but still her lips were moving. I wonder if she talks at school. Something tells me no. If *I'm* worried about going to middle school, I can only imagine how terrified she must be.

I get up from my seat and point to the empty one next to her. "Is it all right if I sit here?"

She nods and gives me a smile. Ollie walks in, and I flag him over to come sit with us. Everyone else takes their usual seats. Hailey is pretty quiet when she walks in. I actually kind of miss her loud mouth. Her stories definitely make things more interesting.

We've finished reading *Wonder* and spend most of the class talking about what happened in the last few chapters. When it's time to go, Ollie's mom is waiting for us right outside the classroom door. She's super tall. I wonder if she was taller than me when she was my age.

"Hello! You must be Sydney," she says. "I've heard so much about you."

"Mom!" Ollie rolls his eyes.

"Hi," I say to her. I look around, hoping no one heard her call me Sydney. "Um, Ollie talks about you too."

She puts her arm around him. "That's sweet."

He winks at me.

"And it's very nice of you to take care of Mr. Toad this weekend," Mrs. Moore tells me. "He's in my van. I parked at the far end of the lot, by the oak tree, so if you have your mom park next to us, we can lift the tank into your car."

I can't wait. I've always wanted a pet. This is going to be a fun weekend. I know turtles aren't cuddly creatures, but I can at least cradle Mr. Toad in my hand or let him sit on my lap, as long as I wash my hands afterward.

As we walk to the front entrance, Mrs. Moore says to me, "Ollie tells me you'll be going to Coral Rock Middle with him this fall."

"Yeah! And Mrs. Wrigley is a counselor there, so we'll get to see her again after the reading class is over." We only have one more week of our summer program, but school starts up again a month after that.

"Too bad Mrs. Wrigley won't be one of our teachers," Ollie says.

I nod. "She really is a good teacher. I hope we don't get any mean ones who pile on the homework until we drown in it."

"I'd pull my eyeballs out, then." Ollie laughs. "But maybe we'll be in some of the same classes, Sydney A."

"That would be really cool, Ollie C." Five days a week with him—no complaints here. "And I'm still not telling you my middle name!"

"I get it, Arlene!"

Mom pulls up to the semicircle as we get outside. I flag her down. "Mom, please pull up to the oak tree. Mr. Toad is here."

"Somebody's excited. And are these Mr. Toad's owners?"

"Yes. This is Mrs. Moore, and this is Ollie."

"Hi, Mrs. Frankel, nice to meet you," says Ollie.

"A pleasure to meet you too. Why don't you all hop in?" Mom drives us over to the oak tree as instructed. "He has such good manners," she whispers to me as she parks next to Mrs. Moore's car.

So embarrassing. I'm not even going to respond.

We all hop out, and our moms chat for a minute. Finally, Mrs. Moore pops her trunk. She and Ollie pull the tank forward a little so we can meet Mr. Toad. Wow, he's a lot bigger than I thought he would be.

"Oh, my goodness!" Mom exclaims.

"Are you okay?" Mrs. Moore asks.

"Ah, yes, but I was expecting an itty-bitty thing." Mom gives me a stern look.

Gulp. "That's what I thought too, Mom." Mr. Toad is no itty-bitty thing. He's way bigger than an eggplant. Bigger than a newborn baby. Almost as big as a skateboard.

Mrs. Moore puts her hands on her hips. "Ollie! You didn't tell them?"

He shrugs. "I guess not. I . . . never really think of him as big."

Mrs. Moore sighs at him. She tells us, "Mr. Toad is a soft-shelled turtle. They grow to the size of their environment. The smaller ones are mud and box turtles. If we had a bigger aquarium, he could've grown up even bigger!" Mrs. Moore waves to Mr. Toad even though he hasn't budged from his shell.

My eyes go wide. I picture a four-foot-long turtle at my kitchen table, slithering up the stairs, sleeping in my bed. It sounds like something out of a movie!

Mrs. Moore turns to Mom. "I feel awful. We'll find him somewhere else to stay if you're not comfortable taking him."

I stare at Mr. Toad. I can't see much because he's inside his shell. "Mom, he's scared." I tug at her sleeve.

Mom gingerly peeks into the tank. "You can leave him with us," she tells Mrs. Moore. Looking at me, she adds, "He'll be okay, Sydney. It's us I'm worried about."

Mrs. Moore laughs. "I really appreciate it. We typed out some instructions, and we've got a bag with his food and any supplies you could possibly need. He's low maintenance, I promise."

After Mrs. Moore goes over the most important instructions with us, we load Mr. Toad into our trunk. It takes three of us—Mrs. Moore, Ollie, and me—to lift the tank, so I'm not sure how we're going to get him out when we get home. But I don't want to scare Mom with any more details. I say goodbye to Ollie and hop into the car.

Mom starts the car and drives off. "This was some surprise!"

I slink down in my seat. "Sorry. I had no idea."

"Mr. Toad seems like a gentle creature, but this is going to be a lot more work than I thought. I think you would've been better off with a box turtle."

"I'll be fine. I'm not a little kid." I grit my teeth. "He can stay with me in my room."

"His tank is too big to get upstairs. We'll keep him in the family room by the big window. He'll have a nice view of our yard. But you'll have to be very thorough about keeping the tank clean and about washing your hands every time you touch him . . ."

The ten-minute ride home seems to take forever. I'm annoyed at Mom for treating me like I can't handle this. But I don't say anything, because I'm afraid that if I do, she'll turn around and bring Mr. Toad back to the Moores.

Mom parks the car and heads straight to the front door.

I stand next to the car. "Hello, Mom! Mr. Toad."

She turns around. "Right, I know. Let me open the front door, and then we can try to get him in."

"But you're not supposed to be lifting heavy things," I say.

"That's true. We should really get someone to help us." She looks at the houses next door, but our neighbors' cars aren't there.

I peek at Mr. Toad and scoop my hands under his belly. "You'll be safe with me," I whisper.

Mom flags down a couple of teenagers who are walking down the street. They help me carry the tank inside.

"Cool pet!" one of the older girls says as she steadies the tank with her knee.

"Thanks." I smile.

The girls leave. I fix up the tank because a few things shifted. Mr. Toad still hasn't popped out of his shell. He's probably shy. I know how he feels. I'll give him some space while he gets used to our house.

"I'll be upstairs. Make sure to check in with the turtle," Mom says.

"That's what I'm doing. I'm just going to make a quick peanut butter sandwich."

"Okay, but wash your hands first, and don't share your food with him."

"I know what to do, Mom," I snap at her and head to the kitchen before she says anything else. She acts as if I've never taken care of *anything* before. We used to have a betta fish when I was little, and I was the one who fed it every morning. Plus, last year I had a kindergarten buddy I read to every week, and her mom said I was very helpful. So I think I can manage a turtle in a tank.

When I come back to the family room, Mr. Toad's still inside his shell. I sit down on the floor and press my face against the tank. "I know how you feel, buddy. It's strange to be in a new place, but I'm a friend of Ollie's."

Mr. Toad slowly pokes his head out. He peers at me with his beady eyes, almost as if he's trying to tell me something. He's looking for some company, I bet.

I run upstairs and search through my old toy box. I pick out my stuffed hippo and run back down.

I place Edna right outside of his tank, facing him.

"Now, listen, Mr. Toad, I know she's not your usual type, but I think you'll get along."

He doesn't move, and obviously neither does Edna.

"You two have a lot in common. You both love mud and water."

He takes one step toward the glass, then another. His head turns to face me and then stops.

"What is it? You can talk to me." I stare straight at him. He looks at Edna, then back at me.

I stand up. "Oh, you want privacy."

I feel you, buddy.

# CHAPTER 26

Mom shakes me awake.

"What's going on?" I ask.

"Someone's hungry."

"No, I'm good." I roll over on my side and smush my pillow over my head.

She tugs at my sheets. "Not you. Aren't you caring for someone?"

I rub at my eyes. "Mom, you're making no sense."

"Mr. Toad is hungry, and you need to feed him!" She sets a basket of unfolded laundry on the floor next to my dresser.

I sit up. "Oh. Why didn't you say that in the first place?"

"I shouldn't have to say anything! This was your idea."

"Relax, Mom! I'm getting up now."

"Don't tell me to relax!" She turns around and huffs toward the door. "I'll see you downstairs."

Geez, Mom is being really annoying. It's not like the turtle is late for work and can't leave until he gets his breakfast.

A couple of minutes later, I join her in the kitchen. I take Mr. Toad's food out of the container in the fridge and put it onto his small feeding tray. Dry pellets and cut-up bits of veggies—not too appetizing, but it looks better than dog food.

"Don't overfeed him," Mom says as she walks by.

"I'm not." I slam the fridge shut and carry the food into the family room. I almost jump when I see his little beady eyes focused on me, his head right up against the glass. Edna, the faithful stuffed hippo, is still pressed up against the other side of the tank.

"Good morning, Mr. Toad. I hope you slept well." I place the tray inside the tank.

He doesn't move.

"Come on. You don't have to be shy with me." I stroke him.

I sit down cross-legged on the carpet in front of the tank. He moves forward a couple of inches but still doesn't touch the food. I'm getting hungry now too. I hope Mr. Toad isn't sick. Can turtles catch colds or get stomachaches like humans? "I'll be right back, Mr. Toad. I'm just going to make myself some breakfast in the kitchen. Holler if you need me."

Okay, that was a stupid thing to say.

In the kitchen, I wash my hands and pour myself a big bowl of cereal. What if Mr. Toad doesn't trust me? He's so used to Ollie, and now he's in this strange house with this strange girl staring at him. What does he do for fun with Ollie? Maybe Mr. Toad needs a good wake-up routine. I rush back into the family room. His food is gone. Well, at least he was hungry.

I play some music on the iPad and stretch back and forth in front of the tank. "Mr. Toad, we're going to get you to loosen up. A few stretches will get your blood pumping. At least that's what my PE teacher says."

I move back and forth like we do at the start of every PE class. Mr. Toad is as still as a rock. He must think I'm nuts. I need a new approach.

Wait! I smack myself on the head. I'm sure Ollie plays with him. I stick my face in the tank. "Mr. Toad, don't be afraid, but I'm going to take you out.

Who wants to stay in a closed space all day?"

I reach under his belly and pull him out. He sneaks back into his shell. I set him down on the carpet and wait for him to poke his head back out. One minute, two minutes, and still nothing. Maybe he doesn't like me.

The phone rings. I don't move, but a second later, Mom calls to me. "It's Maggie!"

"Mr. Toad, I have to take this call. I'll be right back."

Of course, he doesn't bat an eye.

I quickly wash my hands and rush to grab the phone from Mom, who's hovering by the stairs. "When you're done, come to the baby's room," Mom says. "I want to show you a few stencil designs for the wall."

I say okay and get on the phone with Maggie. "What's up?" I ask.

"Do you think I should take guitar lessons?"

I sit down on the top stair. "Why?"

"To play air guitar with Warren."

"Are you serious?"

"Kind of."

I can't help but laugh. "I can just picture you showing up at a guitar lesson with no guitar."

Maggie starts laughing too. "Okay, I guess it's pretty dumb. But I don't want to make a fool out of myself at the school talent show."

"That's not for another few months, so don't worry. And maybe you guys will come up with something else to do anyway." I remember what Dad said when I told him we agreed to go to the race car movie with Warren. "You also don't have to pretend to like things he likes just so he'll like you."

"You're using the word 'like' a lot. Doesn't your mom hate that?"

"Only when it's a filler word. Like, if I was, like, saying it, like, in between, like, every other word as, like, a placeholder."

Mom calls me up to the baby's room.

"Speaking of my mom, I need to help her now, but I'll talk to you later."

I find Mom on the floor with a bunch of stencils laid out. "Which one do you like for the wall border?"

In front of me there are ducks, dogs, sailboats, and turtles. "Turtles?" Oh. Mr. Toad. I forgot about him.

"Turtles? Are you sure?" Mom asks.

"Yes." I rush out of the room and down the stairs. "Mr. Toad," I call. "Sorry I abandoned you . . ."

I run into the family room but don't see him anywhere. "Is this your idea of a joke? Because I don't like it!"

Maybe he's stuck somewhere. I lie down on my stomach and check under the couch and the entertainment center. No sign of him. And really, he's way too big to be under those things anyway. He must be in the kitchen.

Nope. Dining room and bathroom are a nope too. This is kind of nuts. He was stiff as a rock when I ran upstairs, and now he's vanished into thin air. Ollie didn't tell me that Mr. Toad was Turtle Houdini!

Ugh, Ollie. He'll be back to pick up Mr. Toad tomorrow. I have barely twenty-four hours to find Mr. Toad. I hope he's okay!

I plunk down in a kitchen chair. Oh, I'm doomed. I can't even take care of a turtle. If Mom finds out that Mr. Toad is missing, she'll be so mad. She'll never trust me with the baby.

I get up from the table and go back through the rooms again. Seriously, how stupid can I be to leave a pet unattended?

To be fair, turtles aren't known for their speed. I wasn't away for that long, so he couldn't have gone far.

Mom waddles down the stairs holding the turtle stencils. She stops on the last stair to catch her breath. "I'm craving Italian. How about we go to Joe's for lunch?"

"Um, sure . . ."

"Okay, I'll grab my purse. Be back in a minute."

A minute? I can't find Mr. Toad in a minute. I frantically circle through the rooms again, but it's no use. I'm looking behind the couch for the third time when I see Mom standing in the family room doorway with her arms crossed.

"I'm ready to go." She taps her fingers against the doorframe.

"Well, we can't leave yet." I half cover my face with my hands. "Mr. Toad is missing."

"What was that? You're mumbling."

I throw my hands down. "I said I lost Mr. Toad, okay?"

"Lost him? That's impossible." She walks toward the tank and peers inside. "How—?"

"I didn't mean to! I took him out of the tank to get some exercise, and then I forgot about him when you called me upstairs."

"Forgot about him? You shouldn't have taken him out of the tank in the first place! I thought you were more responsible than this, Sydney."

"Do you have to give me a lecture now, Mom?"

"Who said anything about a lecture?" she huffs. Her eyes have narrowed, and she looks mad, but I'm mad too.

"You're always treating me like a baby, and I'm sick of it!" I stomp my foot.

Mom puts her hand on her hip. "Well, this is not a very good example of your being mature."

"Mom, it was an accident. And besides, it's your fault anyway."

Mom gets red in the face—just like I do so often—and raises her voice. "My fault?"

"Yeah! You called me upstairs to look at the stencils while I was playing with him."

"And you didn't have the common sense to put him back first? Not to mention that he isn't even supposed to be out of his tank."

"Actually, you *did* mention that already," I snap. "I know I messed up. But I've fed him and played with him and made him feel at home." I sniff. "I did everything I was supposed to. I even gave him a friend to keep him company." I look over at Edna.

At her soft little furry body and warm black eyes. If only she were real.

"But his safety is key."

"That's why I'm going to find him, and I don't need your help!" I charge out of the room. I attack the kitchen first, throwing open cabinet doors and drawers. I know Mr. Toad couldn't have climbed inside any of them, but it makes me feel better to do *something*.

When I'm at the dishwasher, I feel Mom's hand on my shoulder. "Sydney, I'm sorry if I treated you like a baby. I just wanted to make sure you knew how much responsibility it was to take care of a living creature."

"Don't you think I know that?" I turn to face her. "It's like you don't even trust me!"

"That's not true. I do trust you, and I can't believe how much you've grown this summer."

"Well, it doesn't seem like it. You're always saying things that embarrass me."

"Like what?" She moves around the kitchen shutting the cabinets and drawers.

"Like when you told Mrs. Pendler and Warren about my class. And then you told them I was shy and nervous about middle school. It's a big deal!"

Mom pauses with her hand on a cabinet door. "I certainly didn't mean to embarrass you. It's not unusual to be nervous before going off to middle school."

"But why did you have to say anything at all? She didn't ask you."

"Oh." Mom frowns, but not in an angry way. More like she's deep in thought. "I guess I should've let you speak for yourself."

"Yeah. That's exactly it." Finally, I've gotten through to her! It only took eleven years. Okay, to be fair, she's only been embarrassing me for about *half* of my life. "And you do realize that Warren's going to be in my school next year, right?"

"Wow. I'm sorry, honey. I honestly didn't realize I was making things awkward for you." She sounds like she means it, but I see her lips starting to curve upward.

"Then why are you smiling?"

"Because I'm happy for you. You've made new friends, and you've spoken up for yourself." She hugs me.

It feels good to have Mom's arms around me, even if her huge belly is in the way. "I'm sorry," she whispers.

"I'm sorry too, Mom. I didn't mean to blow up at you, but I was frustrated with the way you were treating me."

Mom kisses my cheek. "I'm glad you told me."

I could stay like this all day, but I know it's not going to help Mr. Toad.

"We've got a turtle to find." I grab Mom's hand.

She follows me into the family room. We pick up pillows and pull the couch forward just like I did earlier. We do the same thing to the dining room. Seriously, where could an oversized turtle go?

Mom and I split up. Now, if I were a turtle, where would I hide? Definitely not in the bathroom. I don't think turtles care much about hygiene. The only place he probably wants to go is . . . home!

I rush to the foyer, and there he is, under the little table right by the front door, blending in with the brown tile. "Mr. Toad!" I scream.

I pick him up, and he stares straight at me. "I know you miss Ollie, but I promise he'll be back tomorrow. And besides, I'm not that bad, am I?"

Mom rushes over. "I'm so relieved you found him."

I settle him back in his tank. "Let's keep this our little secret, buddy. No need to worry Ollie."

Mr. Toad retreats back into his shell.

"I'll take that as a yes."

\* \* \*

On Sunday, I wake up early and spend the morning watching Mr. Toad in his tank. I don't dare leave him for a second, not even to pee. The doorbell rings, and I give him a quick peck on his shell. "I'm going to miss you, buddy."

Mom opens the door and brings Ollie and Mrs. Moore into the family room. Mrs. Moore tells Mom how hot it was in Naples, and Ollie thanks me for watching Mr. Toad.

"I hope he didn't give you any trouble," Ollie says.

"Oh, no. Never." I shake my head. "He was a perfect gentleman."

Ollie crouches down next to the tank and taps on the glass. "Hi, Mr. Toad. I'm back."

Mr. Toad quickly scuttles toward him. I look over at Edna. I hand the stuffed hippo to Ollie. "Take this with you. Mr. Toad really likes her."

He smiles at Edna. "She is kind of cute. Good choice, Mr. Toad."

Mrs. Moore and Mom head to the kitchen to get

the food containers. I sit down next to Ollie in front of the tank.

"You're lucky to have Mr. Toad. He makes things fun," I say.

"Yeah, but you're going to have a sibling—a person who will actually talk back to you. Mr. Toad is more the silent type." He laughs.

"I don't think I'm going to get much out of the baby for at least a year. It's going to be all crying."

"Not all crying," Ollie assures me. "Babies do giggle and make funny cooing noises. At least my cousin's baby does. It's going to be great. You'll see."

"But how can I be sure?" I stare down at the carpet. "What if I'm not big sister material?"

"Trust me. You're going to be awesome. You took good care of Mr. Toad, didn't you?"

Barely.

Ollie has Edna give Mr. Toad a wave. "Just be yourself, Sydney A."

He makes it sound so simple.

I help Mrs. Moore and Ollie carry the tank to the car. Mom says, "Anytime you go away again, we'd be happy to watch him."

My eyes go wide. "Really? Yay! No offense, Ollie, but I hope you go out of town again soon."

He puts his hands on his hips and pretends to be mad. "Fine, I'll have to face it: Mr. Toad is more popular than me."

I laugh. "It's not easy keeping up with a turtle as cool as Mr. Toad!"

Little does he know just how hard it was.

## CHAPTER 27

"I'm so glad everyone's here today, because we're going to talk about our end-of-the-class production," Mrs. Wrigley says on Monday.

Our what?

"This Friday will be our last day together, and all the summer performance classes will be participating in a showcase in the community center's mini theater. I think there are about eight of us. Dance, choir, judo . . . even the crafts class is doing a puppet show. It'll be a great way to share what you've learned with your families."

My family had better not find out about this.

Mrs. Wrigley says, "I'll break you up into groups for this." She says that Ollie, Mary, and I will be one group, and Calvin, Alice, Sara, and Hailey will be the other.

We move our desks together. Mrs. Wrigley says

she'd like each group to perform a scene from *Wonder* at the showcase. She passes out packets of paper that show examples of how to write a scene as a script, with dialogue and stage directions.

I have to say something to stop this madness. "Um, some of us aren't comfortable performing. Is it okay if we prerecord something?"

Mary nods.

But Mrs. Wrigley shakes her head. "No, this is a readers' theater. You don't have to have everything memorized. You'll be reading straight from your script."

That doesn't make me feel any better! I think I'm going to hurl. Mrs. Wrigley is a traitor. How could she do this to me?

"Remember, this won't be a long performance—about five minutes, tops," adds Mrs. Wrigley. "Just pick a few pages of the book to turn into a script."

"What scene do you want to do?" Ollie asks Mary and me.

He might as well ask me if I want to be dead and buried. Still, I try to calm down and focus. Performing onstage will be scary, but as long as I don't tell Mom and Dad it's happening, they'll never have to know. Maggie won't tell her parents either. The

Steins haven't mentioned the dance showcase to my parents, so I think we're in the clear. This doesn't have to be the end of Frankelstein's world.

Even so, it'll be just as horrifying as the county spelling bee would've been.

I fold my arms against my chest. "I hope I don't freeze up during the performance."

"Think of it like a test run for middle school," Ollie says.

I know he's trying to be helpful, but this is much worse. "It just stinks. Being tongue-tied is so embarrassing. Not to mention turning red in the face."

Ollie looks down at his feet. "You're lucky your problem's not anything permanent."

I instantly regret complaining. "I'm sorry. I must sound like such a brat."

He shrugs. "No, it's okay. We all have our issues. At least, that's what my mom says."

"She's right." I sigh.

"Hey, I've got an idea for our performance," Ollie says. "We could do the Halloween scene."

Mary shakes her head. "Sad," she whispers.

"Yeah, I felt so bad for Auggie in that scene," I say.

"I feel bad for him too, but it's an important scene in the book," Ollie says. "And it means we can wear costumes, which'll solve at least half your problem, Margaret."

Ollie grabs his pen and writes *Margaret = ghost.* "You could turn the color of a ripe tomato, and nobody would know."

Mary takes the pen and writes *Mary = ghost #2.* We all crack up, even Mary. It's weird to hear her laugh. Her voice sounds rusty.

Laughing is contagious, and pretty soon, I'm laughing too. Everyone else catches on and laughs with us—even Mrs. Wrigley. She tells us all to stand up, shake our bodies, and let our giggles flow. This makes us crack up even more, and all of a sudden, we're like a bunch of dancing hyenas. I almost wish Mom would walk in right now. We probably look like a real dance class.

\*\*\*

On the drive home, Mom says, "Guess what? I called the community center today."

My heart drops. "Why?"

"Because I wanted to see if I could come and watch your class, since this is the last week."

"Mom, that would be so embarrassing!" I say.

"Relax, Sydney. Turns out most classes have a performance for parents on the last day."

That's it—we're dead. My heart might as well be inside my shoe. Show over. Curtain closed.

"Most classes?" Maggie asks. "What about reading?"

"Yes, I asked about that for your parents. That's one of the most exciting ones." Mom gets out of the car, and we follow right behind her, not wanting to miss a word.

"How can it be exciting? They just read," I say. Maybe I can still get us out of this somehow.

"They put on a short play. Like a readers' theater. Sounds delightful."

We are so dead.

"It'll be lovely to see the product of all your work." Mom rubs her hands together. "Now, who's ready for lunch?"

We both say yes, because otherwise Mom will definitely think something is up. "Wonderful. I ordered a pizza, and I baked cookies."

We don't deserve this. Mom should be feeding us mush with a side of toilet water.

"Thanks, Mom!" I force myself to smile. I'm officially the worst daughter ever.

"Enjoy the food," I whisper to Maggie. "This may be our last supper."

After we're done, we hole up in my room.

As soon as we shut my bedroom door, I whisper frantically, "Mom knows about the performance! That means your parents will know too! We're going to be grounded for life!"

"How could we be so stupid?" Maggie balls up her fists. "Let's just switch back."

"How?"

"We tell the teachers that our classes got mixed up by mistake. Like our parents changed their minds at the last minute or something."

"But if we do that, you'll have to perform with the reading class, and I'll have to perform with the dance class."

"You're not such a bad dancer." Maggie playfully elbows me. "And I can teach you some steps."

"I don't think I'll look convincing enough to fool our parents."

"Well, what else can we do?"

"What if you stay with dance and I stay with reading, but we perform in costumes so no one can tell us apart?"

Maggie stares at me. "Have you seen yourself

lately? Specifically, have you seen how much taller you are than me? No costume can hide that!"

"What about a ghost costume?" I pull the top sheet off my bed and throw it over my head. "Can you still tell it's me?"

"That's stupid." Maggie yanks the sheet off my head.

"Hey, I was getting used to sheet living. But it was kind of hard to breathe under there. Never mind."

"Maybe we should just tell our parents the truth. Get it over with now."

"No! Then they'll never give us phones!" I cry.

"You're right." Maggie flops down onto my carpet. "I really want my own phone. I already picked out a case at the mall too. It's the cutest koala face. But if we tell our parents now, we could do tons of chores to make up for lying to them. Then maybe they'd still let us have our phones."

"I don't know. My mom has been stressed, and stress can hurt the baby. I don't want her to have to go back on bed rest." I cover my face with my hands. "Ugh. This is the worst trouble we've ever been in."

Maggie plops down onto my carpet. "Yeah, much worse than when we ate a whole box of Oreos and hid the empty box under your couch."

"Definitely worse. There has to be a solution."

"We could both pretend to get the flu."

I fake-gag. "I'm not going to sit in a doctor's office around a bunch of sick people and risk *actually* getting sick."

"Yeah, that would be nasty."

"Plus, me being sick could stress out my mom."

Maggie throws her hands up in the air. "I know it might be a shocker, but I'm out of ideas."

I pace around my room. I have to come up with something. "Wait a minute, Maggie. I've got it! Your group and my group could *combine* our performances. That way, we'll be onstage at the same time."

"How are we going to pull that off?"

"Let's come up with the best idea ever and convince our teachers to let our groups merge. If kids from both classes are performing together, no one will be able to tell who's in reading and who's in dance."

"Hmm." Maggie considers for a moment. "This plan is so devious. But yet so genius! I didn't know you had it in you, Syd."

I take a bow. "Why, thank you! I'll consider that a compliment."

"I think Ms. Pat would say yes, actually. She's super relaxed."

"Perfect! I know Mrs. Wrigley will say yes."

Maggie stands up and high-fives me. "Frankelstein, this just might work!"

And if not, we can pick out our jail cells.

"But what should our performance be about?" I ask. "My group was planning to do the Halloween scene from *Wonder.* Do you think your dance group would be okay with that? You could watch the movie. That way you'll know what the story is about."

Maggie smiles. "Actually, I read the whole book."

"You did? That's awesome!" Maggie never finishes a book.

"Yeah, it was so good! I couldn't put it down. I felt like all the characters were real people."

Maybe this isn't going to be such a disaster after all.

## CHAPTER 28

It's taken us all afternoon, but Maggie and I have worked out some dance moves that should work for our performance. Maggie's taught me basic steps from a few different dance styles that her class has learned.

I'm trying not to focus on how nervous I am about actually performing. Instead, I'm concentrating on keeping our switcheroo a secret. We only have one plan: Plan A. There is nothing else to fall back on.

In the morning, Maggie comes with me to talk to Mrs. Wrigley a few minutes before class starts.

Mrs. Wrigley's at her desk reading the newspaper. I didn't know people did that anymore. Mom and Dad get all their news online.

"Hi, Mrs. Wrigley. This is my best friend, Sydney," I say. It's so weird to call somebody else my name. But if I had to choose anyone else to be me, it would definitely be Maggie.

She puts down the paper. "Nice to meet you, Sydney. How can I help you girls?"

I cross my fingers behind my back.

"We wanted to know if we could combine our performances. She's in the dance class." I gesture to Maggie. "And we thought it would be fun for our groups to work together."

"That's a lovely idea. The more the merrier, I say. Fine with me as long as it's okay with Ms. Pat and, of course, your group members."

"Awesome! Thanks." I uncross my fingers. That was easier than I thought. Halfway there.

I turn to Maggie. "Do you want me to come with you to talk to Ms. Pat?"

"Nah, I'm sure she'll be cool with it. I'll come by and update you after I've talked to my group."

I ask Ollie and Mary if they're okay with our plan, and they both immediately say yes. "As long as I don't have to dance, I'm in," Ollie says.

"I promise, you won't have to," I say. "We'll have some parts that are all dancing, some parts that are all speaking, and some parts that are both." Maggie and I will have to do both if we want to fool our parents. But our group members don't need to know that.

Within five minutes, Maggie knocks on the door.

"Can I get it?" I ask Mrs. Wrigley.

She nods.

I poke my head out. "Well?"

"Everyone said yes." Maggie beams.

I give her a thumbs-up. "Same here."

"I have a good feeling about this."

"I don't know if I'd go that far."

"Come on—it'll be fun. Ms. Pat said she'll send our group over here after break so we can start working together right away."

Later, when Maggie's group shows up, we move to the back of the room where there's more space. There are eight of us altogether, three boys and five girls. Ollie takes out the script that he, Mary, and I started writing yesterday. He passes it around so that Maggie's group members can look at it.

"There are only three speaking parts," one of the dance girls says.

"We can break up some of the dialogue and add more lines if more people want to talk," I say. "But if any of you don't want to speak, you don't have to."

Kind of funny: If I had taken the dance class,

I wouldn't have to talk. Mom's mission would've backfired completely.

We end up rewriting the script so that it has six speaking roles.

"Who wants to be Auggie?" Ollie asks.

"I think you should," I say.

Mary ekes out a "Yes."

Ollie agrees.

We divide up the rest of the parts. Mary surprises me and doesn't take the smallest part.

Next, we pick spots in the script where we can have some dancing in between the dialogue. Once we've assigned people to each dancing part, Ollie and Mary and I write out extra copies of the script while the kids from the dance class create their mini routines. Our group is busy nonstop until Mrs. Wrigley says it's time to go.

She comes up to me after class. "Margaret, I'm proud of you for spearheading this group performance. You've really come out of your shell."

No one has ever said that to me before. It feels good—even if my name's not Margaret. "Thank you."

She squeezes my shoulder. "Your parents are going to be very proud too."

I bet.

"See? This *is* fun," Maggie says as we walk out of the building.

"Yeah, I guess you're right. But I hope we don't mess up." I sigh.

"We won't. We've got everything covered." She drapes her arm around my shoulder. "Frankelstein power forever!"

When we get into the car, Mom says, "I've got a surprise for you."

I lean against the front seat. "What?" We're flying to New York tonight and will miss the show?

"Bubbe and Zayde are coming to your performance on Friday."

"What?" My mouth drops. "Why would they want to do that?"

"I thought you'd be happy to see them." I catch Mom's frown in the rearview mirror. She looks shocked.

"I am. It's just that . . ." Hold on while I dig myself out of this hole. "The performance isn't a big deal. Are they sure they want to drive four hours for that?"

"Of course. They don't want to miss the chance to see you onstage."

"But the parents will have to sit in folding

chairs—the hard metal kind without padded seats. You know how Zayde complains about having a sore tuchus from hard chairs."

Okay, maybe that was a tad overboard.

"That's okay, honey," Mom says. "They won't mind. They're excited to see you dance."

Maggie squeezes my hand. "Like I said, we've got this."

I'm not so sure about that, but one thing I do know is that there's no going back.

## CHAPTER 29

We practice with both groups for the next two days. I only have a few lines, so there's not too much to memorize. But I do go over my part of the dance routine a bunch of times. I think the years of playing Dance Showdown in my bedroom with Maggie have paid off. I seriously consider trying to make the ghost costume work, but instead, I settle for last year's Halloween costume, a witch's outfit. It'll be much easier to dance in that than in a long sheet.

As soon as we get to the community center on Friday, our teachers bring us to the mini theater, where we all gather backstage.

I try to do Mom's breathing exercises while the other classes go out onstage one by one.

First, I close my eyes. Then I slowly inhale through my nose and exhale through my mouth. While you're doing the exercises, you're supposed to focus on something. I focus on not throwing up.

"Are you all right, Syd? Because now's not the time to black out on me!" Maggie shakes my shoulder.

"Yeah, I'm just trying to relax before we go onstage."

"Okay, if you say so."

"Try it with me."

Maggie joins me in the breathing. We have a good thing going until Mrs. Wrigley interrupts us. She has the reading class—plus Maggie's group— gather in a circle.

"I'm so proud of each and every one of you," she tells us quietly. "People usually think of reading as a solitary activity, but I see it as a community activity. Whether it's through book discussion or readers' theater, it's a great way to connect with others."

"Is she always like this?" one of the guys from dance whispers.

"Shh." I give him the stink eye.

"Geez," he grumbles.

Our group is the last act in the show, the grand finale—or, depending on how you look at it, the grand disaster. We watch from the wings while the other classes perform.

The singing class is really good. They sing most of their songs a cappella. My other favorite act is the bucket drummers. I never knew pounding on a bunch of orange paint buckets could sound that good.

Hailey, Alice, Calvin, and Sara are up right before us. They do a scene from Auggie's first day at Beecher Prep. Calvin reads Auggie's lines, and this is the most serious I've ever seen him. Hailey wears a fake mustache and reads Mr. Tushman's lines with a lot of flair.

When they get off the stage, they're all beaming.

"You guys were awesome," I say.

They all thank me. Calvin shouts, "Broadway, here we come!"

He cracks me up.

"Okay, Team Reading Dance, you're up," Mrs. Wrigley says.

"I'm nervous," Mary whispers to me.

"Don't worry. I'm nervous too," I say.

But I can honestly say I'm more nervous about not blowing our cover than about actually being onstage.

Before our performance starts, Mrs. Wrigley and Ms. Pat step onto the stage.

"I'm so proud of our students this year," Mrs. Wrigley says. "They're such out-of-the-box thinkers.

I've never had two groups combine performances before, but it's a fabulous idea. This last group will also be performing their interpretation of a scene from the book *Wonder* by R. J. Palacio. The themes are being true to yourself and always treating others with kindness."

Unless you're a gigantic liar. I peek from behind the curtain and see Mom, Dad, Bubbe, and Zayde in the audience. They have huge smiles on their faces, and I haven't even stepped onstage yet. My guilt-o-meter is through the roof. I just have to get through the next five minutes, and then I can finally go back to my un-lying self.

Since Ollie is playing Auggie, he takes the stage first with the girl playing Via, his sister.

Ollie doesn't even need to look at his script. He's a natural.

Maggie and I are behind the curtain on the left side of the stage. "I can't even look at the audience. Is the place full?" Maggie asks.

I take a step forward and pull the curtain back slightly. "It's pretty full. Probably like fifty people."

"Ugh, I wish we could turn back time."

"Me too." But if I did that, I never would've met Mrs. Wrigley. Or Ollie. Or Mary.

Maggie sighs. "This will all be over in like ten minutes."

"Five, but who's counting?" My stomach revs up like an engine. "I'm not feeling great."

"Too late!" Maggie tugs my arm. "We're on."

I follow her onstage, and we launch right into our dance routine. When that's done, it's time for some dialogue.

My first line is about treating others like you want to be treated. I say it without looking at my family.

Ollie is awesome as Auggie. He puts a lot of feeling into his lines. The boy who plays his classmate Jack is really good too. In this scene, he's being mean to Auggie, and it's so convincing that I kind of want to punch him in the face.

We all deliver the last line of our script together. That was Maggie's idea. I thought it was going a little overboard, but Maggie assured us that the adults would love the corniness.

As the audience claps wildly, Mrs. Wrigley steps back up onto the stage. "Thanks so much. Before you leave the stage, will each of you introduce yourselves and say which class you're in?"

This was not part of the plan.

Ollie goes first. People clap again when he says his name. Next are a bunch of kids from the dance class.

My stomach is doing its own tap dance. Out in the audience, Bubbe looks like she's about to cry happy tears. I'm drowning in guilt.

"We have to tell the truth," I whisper to Maggie.

"Now?"

"Yes."

"But the classes are done!" she says through gritted teeth. "If you say you took dance and I say I took reading, and we get our families out of here before the teachers can ask any questions, our parents never have to know."

"But we aren't being true to ourselves." If I can't do that, how am I going to be a good big sister? I take a slow, deep breath like I practiced earlier.

It's Mary's turn. She actually says her name loud and clear. I'm so happy for her. I peer over at Mrs. Wrigley, and she's all smiles.

"But what about our cell phones?" Maggie pleads.

Mary's holding the microphone, ready to pass it to me.

I exhale. "Maybe we'll be out of the doghouse in time for Hanukkah."

I take the mic with one hand and squeeze Maggie's hand with the other. "My name is Sydney Ahuda Frankel," I say. "I was in Mrs. Wrigley's reading class."

Everyone onstage gapes at me. I've never seen Mrs. Wrigley look so shocked.

"Maggie and I traded places," I continue. "We each wanted to be in the other class, but our parents wouldn't let us. So we switched. We're sorry we lied to everyone, especially our parents."

No one knows what to do. The audience is staring. That's like a hundred eyes. I spot Jake sitting with Maggie's parents. I'm glad I didn't notice him before, or I would've been even more nervous. Surprisingly, he's not even laughing at us.

I squeeze Maggie's hand and continue, "But it turns out we were in the right places. I learned so much from Mrs. Wrigley. She helped me face my fears and speak up for myself. I don't think I could've gotten up here without hyperventilating and turning red if it wasn't for her."

I angle the mic toward Maggie, and she leans over to speak into it. "I'm Maggie Stein, and I really loved the dance class. I'm definitely joining my middle school dance team in the fall. And even though

I wasn't in the reading class, I read the book *Wonder* in three days. It was that good. The last whole book I read by myself was a picture book." She lets out a nervous laugh.

Silence.

Bubbe stands up clapping, followed closely by Zayde. Soon, more people stand up—including Mom and Dad and Maggie's parents. Before you know it, everyone in the room is applauding.

I know my face is probably red, but I'm still standing up here up on the stage in front of all these people. And amazingly, I feel pretty calm.

We're probably still in trouble with our parents, but that doesn't feel so scary anymore. Mom doesn't look stressed or even upset. She's actually smiling.

I bring the mic back to Mrs. Wrigley, who looks surprised but happy. I give her a hug. "This was the best class ever," I whisper to her.

Finally, I turn to Ollie. "Ahuda. *A-h-u-d-a*. It means *dear one* in Hebrew."

"That's much cooler than Cable." He smiles. "It means *rope*."

I smile too.

When I step off the stage, Mom and Dad are waiting for me on the side. Mom has tears in her eyes.

"I didn't mean to lie to you," I whisper. "I *wanted* to tell you the truth. But I was afraid it would stress Mom out."

"Oh, Sydney," says Dad, "when we've talked about keeping Mom's stress to a minimum, we never meant you should hide your own problems and worries."

"I'd be *more* stressed if I thought you were keeping things from us!" adds Mom. She squeezes my hands. "You should always feel comfortable coming to us when something's bothering you. I'll try to be better at listening."

"We love you very much, *sheyne meydl*," Dad says.

They both throw their arms around me, and I know they mean it.

This may have been the biggest mix-up of my life, but I wouldn't change a thing.

# ACKNOWLEDGMENTS

It may only take one person to write a story, but it takes many people to publish a book. Sydney Frankel and her friends were with me for some time before they made it to the pages of this book. A lot of people have helped along the way, and for that I am eternally grateful.

First of all, I want to thank my editor, Amy Fitzgerald—a true pleasure to work with—for her guidance. A special thanks to Joni Sussman for bringing me on board and to the rest of the staff at Lerner for all your hard work.

Thanks to my agent, Susie Cohen, for believing in this story.

To everyone at PJ Our Way and the TENT program, I'm grateful to you for allowing me the space to workshop my story amongst my peers.

Thanks to my South Florida critique group members and my writing buddies: Christina Diaz Gonzalez, Gaby Triana, Alexandra Flinn, Alexandra Alessandri, Stephanie Rae, Linda Bernfeld, Adrienne Sylver, Laurie Friedman, and Joanne Levy. Your insight and friendship are paramount.

Thanks to the following experts in their fields for answering my technical questions: Meredith Adams, Robert Blackgrove, and Hilary Leamer. Also, thanks to Ro and Allison for your support and enthusiasm, and to the Cohen fam for providing me many childhood memories to cherish and draw from.

A heartfelt thanks to my husband, Delle, and my kids, Marley, Makhi, and Naya, for helping make all of this possible by always supporting me and being my sounding board.

## ABOUT THE AUTHOR

Danielle Joseph was born in Cape Town, South Africa. The author of several young adult novels and picture books, she lives in Maryland with her husband, three kids, and a dog named Ringo. When not writing, she's swimming, listening to music, or chasing after her dog!